SWEPT AWAY

SWEPT AWAY

RUTH MORNAY and the UNWANTED CLUES

Natalie Hyde

DCB

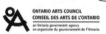

The publisher gratefully acknowledges the support of the Canada Council
for the Arts and the Ontario Arts Council for its publishing program.
We acknowledge the financial support of the Government of Canada through
the Canada Book Fund (CBF) for our publishing activities, and the
Government of Ontario through Ontario Creates, an agency of the Ontario
Ministry of Culture, and the Ontario Book Publishing Tax Credit Program.

LIBRARY AND ARCHIVES CANADA CATALOGUING IN PUBLICATION

Title: Swept away : Ruth Mornay and the unwanted clues / Natalie Hyde.
Other titles: Ruth Mornay and the unwanted clues
Names: Hyde, Natalie, 1963- author.
Identifiers: Canadiana (print) 20220478732 | Canadiana (ebook) 20220478759 |
ISBN 9781770866898 (softcover) | ISBN 9781770866904 (HTML)
Subjects: LCGFT: Novels.
Classification: LCC PS8615.Y33 S94 2023 | DDC JC813/.6—dc23

United States Library of Congress Control Number: 2022951928

Cover art: Julie McLaughlin
Interior text design: Tannice Goddard, tannicegdesigns.ca
Manufactured by Friesens in Altona, Manitoba in February, 2023.

DCB Young Readers
AN IMPRINT OF CORMORANT BOOKS INC.
260 ISHPADINAA (SPADINA) AVENUE, SUITE 502, TKARONTO (TORONTO), ONTARIO, M5T 2E4
www.dcbyoungreaders.com
www.cormorantbooks.com

For Nathan,
who is always willing to float some ideas to me

◈ Chapter 1 ◈

The day Beatrice Payens went missing, the wide-brimmed hat she always wore was found tangled among the thorns of a shrub rose along the banks of the Teeswater River. That turned out to be the only clue to her disappearance. Despite a search lasting three weeks and involving over two hundred people, more than the entire population of Pinkerton seeing as volunteers from the two nearest villages were called in, Beatrice was never seen again.

"Swept away," Mr. Weeks said, surveying the damage done by the river ripping and clawing at the bank. "Stupid beavers used punky wood to build their dam and it gave way. You'd think she, of all people, would know better." He shook his head. Ruth wasn't sure whether he was shaking his head at the beavers using rotten wood or the fact that Beatrice, who was the head of the Teeswater River Embankment Rehabilitation Society, would be so careless as to walk there this time of year. In the end, it was Mr. Weeks's statement of having seen sixty-three-year-old Beatrice Payens staggering along the bank the afternoon of her disappearance and the hat that Ruth had found that left no doubt in anyone's mind, including the local police, of her tragic end.

Ruth expected to feel something at the official notice that her body had been found — after all, despite the fifty-two years difference in their ages, Bea was her friend. But Ruth felt nothing ... not even anger toward the beaver.

Ruth watched as Bea's house sat still and quiet for two months until the day a Rent-All truck pulled in to its driveway and a thin man with hunched shoulders and a young boy with no expression got out and moved some things into the house.

Ruth wondered who they were. Bea hadn't mentioned relatives.

Ruth watched from her perch high in the maple tree across the street the next afternoon as Mrs. Gorgonzola waddled over with a casserole dish held by two enormous pot holders that looked like lobster claws. Mrs. Gorgonzola was the type who wouldn't rest until she knew who those two people were who were moving things into Beatrice's house.

Ruth kept watching although she didn't like to think that she was as nosy as Mrs. Gorgonzola, whom she secretly despised for spreading gossip, especially as it often seemed to be about her own family. Ruth had discovered that Mrs. Gorgonzola called Ruth's parents "those New Age hippies who give no thought to global overpopulation by having seven children." Ruth got the distinct impression that in Mrs. Gorgonzola's eyes, six children was simply a healthy commitment to marriage, as she herself was one of six sisters, but that the seventh child had tipped the scales, and Ruth, as the youngest and the seventh, was the child that shouldn't have been.

Mrs. Gorgonzola's disapproving looks were severe and somewhat exhausting to endure, so over time, Ruth became quieter and smaller and had felt herself slowly disappearing to avoid them. It helped that Ruth had mousy brown hair, brown eyes, no freckles, and no dimples — nothing that would make her stand out. She was as plain as a fence post, as Harriet Ings was fond of saying. Ruth had perfected this disappearing so much that most of the people in the hamlet of Pinkerton hardly realized she was there anymore. Even her own parents sometimes didn't notice she hadn't come down from the maple tree and they would pile into the second-hand minibus and go on an outing to the Perth Garlic Festival or the Annual Salamander Count without her.

Ruth didn't mind. In fact, she preferred being by herself. Ruth didn't feel the need to surround herself with hordes of people. She preferred one amazing friend to lots of mediocre friends, and Beatrice had been that one friend. And besides, being almost invisible had its advantages. She overheard things because those doing the talking didn't notice she was listening. She saw things because no one noticed her watching. And because of that, she knew things that others didn't.

She had heard things about Bea, mostly spread by Mrs. Gorgonzola — stories about cults, secret identities, and buried treasure. Ruth didn't believe a word of it. If Bea was worshipping turnips by the light of a full moon, or was a double agent, or had a chest of pirate gold on her land, Ruth would have known about it because unlike other people, Ruth wasn't invisible to her. Bea talked to Ruth. She told her stories about her childhood, places she had travelled, and people she had met. They were friends, and friends don't keep secrets from each other. Or at least, that's what Ruth thought.

⁓ Chapter 2 ⁓

"His name is Hugh Rolls," Mrs. Gorgonzola said, leaning over the counter conspiratorially at Sam's Gas 'n' Go. "He called her 'Aunt Bea' so he must be her nephew. It came as a shock to him that he'd inherited the house ... he didn't even know he was in the will."

Harriet Ings' mouth opened slightly as she rang in a dozen eggs.

Mrs. Gorgonzola was pleased with the effect her news was having. It certainly was worth the cost and effort of the chicken artichoke casserole she had taken over.

"Didn't Mrs. Payens have children of her own?" Harriet asked.

Mrs. Gorgonzola looked around to make sure she wasn't overheard. She didn't notice Ruth standing in the snack aisle trying to decide between Hickory Sticks and pork scratchings. A faint whiff of something that smelled like a dead eel convinced Ruth that the pork scratchings had gone rancid. One bag had puffed up so that its seams were strained and looked like it would burst at any moment. The one beside it was deflated with a split seam. It was the source of the smell. Ruth saw the best before date on it was four months past. That was pretty standard for Sam's. Rumor was that the faded box of cream crackers on the top shelf had been there since the store opened in 1957.

"I heard that she wasn't really a *Mrs.* but only a *Miss*, and that she had never married because she was jilted at the altar."

At this Harriet Ings gasped. "How tragic," she said, tsking and shaking her head. Mrs. Ings believed strongly in marriage, which is why people said she kept her married name even though Mr. Ings had run off with a travel agent years ago. "Do you think it's true?"

"At one of the Association of Dressings and Sauces meetings at her house, I happened to see a framed photo of a young man wearing a beret signed, *With deepest affection, Antoine*. It was on the sideboard where I went to find a tissue," she added, not wanting Harriet Ings to think she had been snooping in Beatrice's desk drawer, which she most certainly was.

"What about the boy?" Harriet asked.

"Hugh's son. He is a bit odd and shy. Barely spoke a word to me. Saul is his name. Didn't seem particularly glad to be here."

Ruth straightened her shoulders at that bit of news. While she didn't think Pinkerton was as fascinating and charming as the tourists who drove through the village after making a wrong turn at Highway 27 thought it was, it was certainly nothing to sneer at. And although she wasn't really aware of it, Ruth was already forming a bad opinion of Saul.

Mrs. Gorgonzola took her eggs and left Sam's Gas 'n' Go to make custard for her dessert trifle.

Ruth settled on the Hickory Sticks and went to the counter to pay. Harriet Ings rang her through.

"And what's wrong with living in Pinkerton?" Mrs. Ings asked Ruth, as if they were already in the middle of a conversation. "A small hamlet where people care about each other is infinitely better than a big city with anonymous clerks and rude children. Or is that rude clerks and anonymous children?" she asked herself, handing Ruth her change absently.

As Ruth turned to leave the store she almost bumped into a boy who stood uncertainly in the middle of the aisle as if he didn't quite remember why he had come.

"The pork scratchings have turned," Ruth told him helpfully.

He neither smiled nor frowned at the news, but turned to go down the aisle with pet food and cleaning supplies. He was Saul, of course. That was no mystery to Ruth, who, like everyone in Pinkerton, knew every other person living there. She wondered how someone so miserable and unresponsive could be related to Bea. Bea was one of the happiest and most optimistic people Ruth had ever met.

If she were honest, it bothered Ruth to know there were two strangers living in Bea's house. And Saul hadn't just been silent around Mrs. Gorgonzola, he had barely spoken to anyone in Pinkerton for the whole three weeks he had been living there. He would nod or shrug, depending on his answer to the questions he was asked.

"Isn't he polite?" was the whisper around town. In Pinkerton, speaking your mind was frowned upon. Children were to be seen and not heard. Unless you were Ruth, and then you were heard but not seen.

Ruth had decided to use her invisibility to squash the nasty rumors about Bea. After all, friends protect friends' reputations, even if they were careless enough to walk on a muddy bank and be swept away by an angry spring flood. She would find out the truth and present it to Mrs. Gorgonzola's nosy face. But in that moment, Ruth had forgotten what she had observed by being invisible — and that's that the truth was seldom what we thought it was.

One truth that she learned quickly was that Saul wasn't at all silent like his reputation in Pinkerton, because it was Saul who spoke first when Ruth ventured to locate Dorcas, one of their Rhode Island Red hens, from the ditch in front of Bea's house. Dorcas had decided early on that she preferred to lay her eggs in out-of-the-way places around Pinkerton instead of the warm, cozy nest boxes that Ruth's father had built. Ruth supposed that was because Dorcas was actually a very clever hen and had noticed that when she laid eggs in the nest boxes, they disappeared.

"I wondered when you'd come," Saul said, standing on one side of the ditch, his hands stuffed into the pockets of his jeans.

Ruth couldn't imagine why he thought she would come at all. She had, in fact, been avoiding him.

"Come for what?"

"To collect your things."

Ruth paused, trying to think of what items of hers could possibly be in Bea's house. Had she left something behind on her last visit?

"What things?"

"The things she left you in her will."

Ruth hadn't heard anything about being in Bea's will but then neither had Saul's father, so someone wasn't doing their job. Ruth hoped the "things" she was left didn't include the weird flower picture hanging in Bea's living room. Bea had told her it was made of human hair twisted and braided to form petals and leaves. That sort of thing made

Ruth gag. She hated the very sight of it. Now, the kitten teapot where tea poured out of her upheld paw would be nice. Or maybe her complete collection of Nancy Drew books. Ruth loved reading. And tea. Bea had introduced her to orange pekoe, brewed strong in the kitten teapot, and poured into one of Bea's fancy china tea cups with cream, not milk, and two sugars. One time, Bea had offered her English Breakfast tea, but Ruth turned it down politely saying it was already one o'clock in the afternoon. That had made Bea laugh, although Ruth was never really sure why.

"I can get them now," Ruth said.

Saul's eyes dropped to Dorcas, resting in her arms. "What about her?" he asked.

Ruth looked at Dorcas, who had a smug look on her face that once again she had managed to escape and hide her egg. "She doesn't mind coming with us as long as we don't take forever," Ruth said.

At this Saul turned and headed back up the embankment toward the house. As Ruth followed him onto the porch, she noticed that almost nothing had been touched since Bea had died. The braided rag rug, which Bea had woven herself out of old shirts and tea towels, was still laying in front of her white wicker settee. The tin milk pitcher that Bea had filled with spring daffodils and tulips was still on the wooden table, although the flowers had long since browned and wilted and hung over the edges of the pitcher like swooning actresses in an old silent movie.

Inside, Ruth followed Saul past the living room still full of Bea's wide assortment of furniture, none of which matched — which was what Bea liked about it — and the bookshelves still crammed with her books.

In the dining room, atop the mahogany table where Ruth and Bea had shared so many cups of tea and peanut butter cookies, was a cardboard box.

"Here," Saul said, sliding it toward her.

Ruth and Dorcas peered inside. Ruth could see a small, metal frog with a hose attachment coming out of his butt and holes in his back; a pair of very old, slightly yellowed, embroidered ladies' gloves; and the dreaded human-hair flower picture. Ruth was more than a little disappointed. There wasn't one thing in the box that Ruth had admired or commented on all the times she had been in Bea's house. Not one.

"I don't think this is for me," she said. In her arms, Dorcas clucked in agreement.

"Yes, it is," Saul said.

Ruth peered inside again, and with her free hand, moved the stained gloves aside, hoping to see something pretty or sentimental hidden underneath.

"Nope. Must be some other Ruth." Ruth didn't want to

be rude, but she also didn't want to take home this box of hideous and worthless items.

Saul folded his arms. "You're Ruth Mornay, aren't you?"

It was no use. She couldn't very well pretend she wasn't when every last person in the village knew she was. She was going to have to take possession of the box. "Yes," she said dejectedly. She was surprised that the person she thought had been a close friend, a *confidante*, would leave her such a pile of junk.

Dorcas wiggled in her arms, anxious to be on her way.

"Um, I can't carry both home. Will you hold Dorcas for me?"

Saul picked up the box. "No. I don't do chickens."

Dorcas looked right at him with her beady eyes and gave a low cluck. Ruth paused for a moment. She could see through to the kitchen where the kitten teapot still sat in its usual spot up on the corner shelf by the sink, but she didn't have the nerve to ask for it.

Dorcas wiggled to get down as soon as they were out of the house. They made a strange procession walking down the front path, across the road and down over the bridge to the Mornays' property. Once on their driveway, Dorcas walked sedately to the backyard where a few grains of chicken feed still littered the ground.

Saul handed her the box, his duty done.

"She said you'd know what to do with them."

"She did? When?"

"In the will."

Ruth peered into the box again, wondering if she had missed something. She looked up and smiled as if she understood. As Saul walked back across the creek to Bea's house, Ruth came to the sad realization that the only thing she could think of to do with them was burn them.

⌇ Chapter 3 ⌇

In the end, Ruth didn't burn them. She put the garden-sprinkler frog out in her mother's potting shed, the gloves in her night table, and hung the picture downstairs in the den on an empty nail above their red horsehair sofa. The den walls were the repository for all the weird and wacky art that she and her brothers either made or found at flea markets. Her parents always told their friends that they wanted to develop their kids' love of art and at least in the den, only the family was afflicted with looking at it. And putting it there, at least Ruth wouldn't have to look at it before she went to sleep and have nightmares. Ruth had lots of nightmares. Sometimes she woke up in a sweat, shaking. Sometimes they came true. Ruth didn't tell anyone that. She also never told anyone that one of her nightmares three months ago had been about a drowning. She never thought for a moment that it might be Bea who would drown or she would have said something to warn her. It was a ball of guilt that Ruth carried around in her gut that seemed to get heavier and heavier with each passing day.

"Did you figure out what to do with them?" a voice asked her a few days later as she poked her head under the stone bridge that spanned the creek. It was a favorite spot of Dorcas, who was missing again.

Ruth lifted her head. Saul was leaning over the side of the bridge, his long bangs falling over his eyes.

She couldn't understand what difference it would make to him whether she built a shrine for her inherited junk or had donated them to a charity shop. Or burned them, for that matter.

"Yup," was all she said.

Saul didn't seem satisfied. "Well, what was it?"

Ruth stood up, her eyes narrowed. "What's it to you? I bet you barely knew her."

Saul shoved his hands in his pockets again. "We wrote to each other."

"You did?" This was news to Ruth. Bea had never mentioned him in all the times they had been together. *Why would she keep that from me?* Ruth wondered. *What if she had kept other things from me too?* also crept into her mind.

It was an uncomfortable feeling. She pasted a smile on her face.

"What did you write about?"

Now Saul got cagey. "All kinds of things."

The smile left Ruth's face. She found it exhausting to be pleasant at the best of times, and this wasn't one of those times. She found Saul annoying. And the truth was, she was a little jealous that Bea had been writing to him all that time and had never told her.

"What kinds of things," Ruth asked, folding her arms. She wasn't going to let this go that easily.

Saul laughed. "She said you were stubborn."

Now a shiver went through Ruth. "What else did she say?"

Saul looked uncomfortable. "She said you were really smart …" He let his voice trail off.

"And?"

"And I should make friends with you."

Not many things shocked Ruth. With all she had seen and heard from her maple tree perch, she thought herself pretty steady. But this knocked the wind out of her a bit.

"Why would she say a thing like that? You didn't even live here!"

Saul looked up above her head, out into the distance. "She predicted her death, you know."

No, Ruth didn't know. In fact, she was starting to feel like she didn't know Bea at all.

"And I lied a bit," he added.

"About what?"

"That Aunt Bea left you those things in her will. She didn't."

Ruth gaped. "Then why …?"

"She told me to give them to you in one of her letters. She said you'd understand. She said you'd know what to do with them."

"Sounds like Bea said a lot of things in her letters," Ruth said, with just a hint of bitterness in her voice. Then she heard a soft cluck from the reeds under the bridge. She ducked low and waded on the edge of the creek, soaking her running shoe right through. Ruth hated wet socks. It was just another thing to annoy her. She grabbed Dorcas and hauled her out. "And I have no idea what to do with them," she said.

Saul gave a loud sigh. "Then think. She said you were smart." He turned to go.

"Wait a minute!" Ruth scrambled up from the creek, balancing a squirming Dorcas. "What difference does it make what I do with them? Or whether or not I understand?"

Saul looked straight into her eyes. "Because when Aunt Bea predicted her own death, she said it would be murder."

🙦 Chapter 4 🙤

Ruth sat up in the high limbs of the maple tree to think. She did some of her best thinking there. The leaves were the perfect screen so no one would bug her. Most people bugged her. Her report cards at school always contained the comment, *Does not get along well with others.* The tree allowed her to watch the comings and goings of the 134 people who lived in Pinkerton without having to speak to anyone.

Ruth watched as Saul's father hopped into his car and backed out of the driveway. He took off toward the highway that led south out of town more quickly than most people in Pinkerton drive on the loose gravel road in order to protect their cars from stone chips.

Ruth had to admit it was the perfect time to talk to Saul and get to the bottom of Bea's death. Or murder, if you believe in premonitions. So Ruth climbed down from her perch and took the path through the woods and across the road just north of Bea's house to avoid Mrs. Gorgonzola's prying eyes. She wouldn't want to have to explain why she was visiting Saul with his father not home.

Saul answered the side door and Ruth pushed her way into the kitchen. A few dirty dishes were piled in the sink, but other than that, it was pretty neat.

"She couldn't have been murdered," Ruth blurted out. "I would have known. I didn't dream about murder, I dreamt about a drowning."

Saul closed the door. "Look, I don't know. All I know is, Aunt Bea told me that she was going to die soon, and what I was supposed to do when it happened, and that it would have been against her will."

Ruth slumped into a chair. "I can't believe it."

Saul pulled out a chair for himself. "Neither can I. I thought she was just being dramatic. You know, old people can be, well, a bit obsessed with death. And what do you mean you dreamt about a drowning?"

"I mean, we heard it was just a drowning." Ruth quickly corrected herself. There was no way she wanted to reveal to Saul how some of her nightmares felt so real she wasn't sure whether she was sleeping or awake. And after the really bad ones, she lived in fear for days that she would hear they had happened in real life.

"Tell me again about the items," Ruth asked. 'Why would

she give me such stupid things to remember her by?"

Saul shook his head. "I don't think they're souvenirs. I think they're clues."

"Clues to what?"

"Clues to why she was murdered, of course."

"Look, I think Bea got me confused with Nancy Drew. I'm no detective. I don't follow footprints and get locked in closets or find dead bodies."

They sat in silence for a while.

"Why would Bea think she was going to be murdered, anyway?" Ruth asked. The whole thing sounded ridiculous to her. You could count on certain things, living in Pinkerton. You could count on not having fast Internet, especially after school when it slowed to a crawl as every last kid in town went online while pretending to do homework. And you could be sure that any dog smaller than a raccoon left outside unguarded would be a hawk snack. And you could count on the biggest excitement in town being the riding lawnmower race on Thanksgiving weekend. But mostly you could count on the fact that people didn't get murdered in Pinkerton.

"She wasn't really," Saul said.

"Murdered?"

"My aunt."

Ruth threw her hands up in the air. "Has anything you've said been true?"

"I never told you she was my aunt."

"You called her 'Aunt Bea.'"

"Yeah, but she was an honorary aunt. Not a blood relative. I think she was my dad's godmother or something and we just always called her Aunt Bea."

Ruth's eyes narrowed. Now things really didn't make sense. Bea left her house and all her belongings to people she wasn't even related to? And she gave Saul all these instructions about what to give her? Why wouldn't Bea just tell her those things herself?

"Show me the letter," Ruth said, folding her arms.

Saul flushed. "I don't have it anymore."

"How convenient," she said, unable to hide her sarcasm.

Saul ran a hand through his hair. "Look, she told me to burn the letters after I read them."

"What were they? Mission Impossible instructions? And then how are you even sure those were the things I was meant to have? Did you write them down?" Visions of the kitten teapot floated across her mind.

"I didn't need to," Saul said. "I have an eidetic memory."

"An eye what?"

"Eidetic. Like a photographic memory. I see images of

things even long after they're gone. I know *exactly* what that letter said."

Ruth was torn between two possibilities. One was that Saul was lying, in which case Bea didn't actually write to him or predict her own death and he was just pranking her by giving her those oddball items. Or two, that Saul was telling the truth. In that case, Bea must have held deep secrets — deep and dark enough to be murdered. And those hideous items? They must really be clues.

Ruth pushed back her chair and stood up to leave. She felt sure Bea would have hinted at something if she thought her life were in danger and would have given her some instructions herself. That's the kind of friendship they had. As Ruth put her hand on the doorknob, she made a decision. She spun around.

"Do you drink tea?" she asked Saul.

Saul made a face. "No."

"Does your dad?"

"He's strictly a coffee man."

"So you wouldn't mind then if I took that teapot?" Ruth asked, pointing at the kitten teapot and holding her breath.

"Go ahead."

Ruth went to the shelf by the sink and gently took down the one thing that reminded her most of Bea. She tucked it under her arm. As she went out the door she said, "By the way, I don't believe you."

Ruth slipped back home through the woods, invisible to everyone except Dorcas who raised her head as Ruth crossed their backyard. Safe in her room, Ruth carefully set the teapot on her dresser. For the first time since Bea died, Ruth cried.

❧ Chapter 5 ❧

The sky was moody for July. The forecast called for showers and high winds. Ruth liked stormy days. She loved watching the gray clouds gather and boil until they spilled over and pounded the earth with rain. Her maple tree would have been an ideal perch to watch the coming storm roll in except the strong winds made even the sturdy branches of the eighty-year-old tree sway and the swaying made Ruth motion sick. Just about everything made her motion sick: cars, buses, trains, boats, carnival rides, hammocks, swing sets. So she was forced to sit inside and decided the only thing to do was to curl up on the red horsehair sofa with a book to wait it out. She picked *Anne of Green Gables* for the hundredth time, tucked her feet under her, and prepared to disappear into Anne's world. But reading was impossible when her six older brothers took turns swarming like deerflies and teased and nagged and poked her until she felt her nerves as taut as violin strings.

Tea is good for the nerves Bea used to say when Ruth would come over after a particularly trying day at school when her invisibility wore thin and she had to deal with people. Ruth flung the book on the sofa and pushed her way past George and Abe who were wrestling for the remote, and went upstairs to her room to fetch the kitten teapot. It had been two weeks since she had taken it from Bea's house, but today, with Bea's words fresh in her mind, it seemed the right time to finally use it.

She remembered what Bea had taught her about making tea — that before she poured the boiling water in, she needed to warm the teapot. Back in the kitchen she opened the lid and tipped the teapot over into the sink, in case anything had crawled in there. Abe didn't always keep the lid on his ant farm tightly closed. A small piece of white paper fluttered out. Ruth set the teapot down and fished it out of the sink. It was folded in half and inside was a delicate handwriting that Ruth knew so well.

As she read the note, she heard a low buzzing in her ears, everything dimmed, and she felt her knees buckle. She grabbed at the edge of the counter to steady herself, knocking a glass onto the floor, where it shattered.

"Ruth? Ruth, are you okay?" her mother called from the dining room in a voice that seemed to Ruth to be far away.

Ruth hadn't exactly fainted, but it was close. She felt her

mother leading her to the sofa in the den and making her lie down.

"Dehydrated. That's what you are," her mother said, pinching and pulling up the skin on her arm to check. "No tea for you. Water. And lots of it. Now start drinking."

Ruth didn't protest but took a long gulp of water from the glass her mother had fetched from the kitchen. Ruth nodded in order to reassure her mother that she was fine so that she would go away and Ruth could reread the note that was still clutched in her right hand.

"You don't get this frailness from *my* side of the family," her mother said, pursing her lips. "The Sharpes are tough as nails. Your great-aunt Berta flew fighter jets in World War II and your great-grandmother Eusemar sailed her father's schooner to rescue more than half the crew from where they were stranded on the rocks near Ragged Cove."

Just picturing a plane bucking and diving on the wind or a schooner rolling on huge waves began to make Ruth feel woozy again. It was a sad fact that Ruth could become motion sick just by *thinking* of the world moving under her feet.

"All Mornay," her mother sighed.

"I'm feeling much better," Ruth told her, struggling to sit up.

"Lie here and drink," her mother said, "but not at the same time. That's dangerous. Sit to drink and then lie down again."

It was a good thing Ruth *was* lying down as she uncrumpled the piece of paper in her hand and reread it. The shock was almost as bad the second time around.

Don't blame Saul, I forgot to include this in his letter.

It wasn't just the emotion of seeing Bea's handwriting again that affected Ruth so much, or the fact that Bea had somehow known that she would take the kitten teapot. It was the realization that Saul had been telling the truth. Bea *had* been writing to him. She *had* left him instructions in the letter. And Bea *had* predicted her own end.

Ruth tried to channel Nancy Drew. What exactly do you do when you learn your close friend has been murdered? There wasn't any evidence to take to the police; all there was, was a tale of a premonition and some ashes that used to be a letter. There was no body, no murder weapon, and no motive. She would be laughed right out of the police station.

Ruth faced an uncomfortable reality — she was going to have to work with Saul, the boy she had falsely accused of lying to her. The one who annoyed her. The one she was jealous of because of his close relationship with Bea, where he was entrusted with important information and not her. Ruth did her best to push those feelings away and focus on the fact that Bea somehow thought that the two of them could and would avenge her death. There was no way Ruth was going to let her friend down.

The storm outside unleashed its fury and rain drove horizontally at the windows. She took another swig of water and lay back on the sofa to think. A sudden gust of wind blew open the back door and roared through the house. Ruth looked up just in time to see the hair picture come crashing down. She instinctively tried to roll to the side to avoid the glass smashing her in the face, felt it hit her on the shoulder and then it landed face down on her chest.

"Are you drinking your water?" her mother called from the kitchen as she slammed the back door shut again.

"Yes. My eyeballs are floating. Can I get up now?"

"As long as you keep drinking."

Ruth sat up and flipped the picture over on her lap. It was just as ugly up close as it was hanging on a wall. As she studied it, she could see from the yellowed background fabric that it was very, very old. She also noticed that each petal was a tightly braided oval that circled a French knot of hair. The petals, leaves, and stems were different patterns of twists and knots, and they all seemed to be slightly different shades and thicknesses as if they had come from different people. Ruth shuddered at that. In fact, as she looked closer, she realized there must have been hundreds of people's hair in there.

"Eww," she said, throwing the picture onto the sofa beside her. She couldn't imagine who in their right mind thought this would be a fun arts and crafts project. Didn't people have thread or wool back then that they could have used, she wondered? She picked up her book and tried to read but it was no use. She was drawn to the picture like a magnet. She picked it up again, trying to understand how it could be a clue.

She tried holding it closer, then farther away, then crossing her eyes to see if there was a message in the pattern of lines and circles. Nothing. She tried counting the number of petals versus leaves for a formula or binary code or something. Nothing.

Ruth did notice that each braid or twisted strand of hair had been sewn in place … with more hair, except for one petal near the top of the photo, which had been glued. Ruth could see how the glue had seeped through the material. The petal was made of a tiny light brown braid, but it wasn't done as carefully as the others. Some small ends stuck out and the oval was a little lopsided, like it had been done in a hurry. The flower, too, had a couple of empty spots as if it were missing petals.

Ruth hung the picture back on the wall feeling down, defeated, and not at all as smart as Bea seemed to have thought she was.

༺ Chapter 6 ༻

It was a chore she was dreading, but Ruth knew she owed Saul an apology. It was not something she had to do often, as Ruth was actually very seldom wrong. She wondered if Saul were the type to gloat. Still, she wanted to make a good job of it, so she practiced her speech in front of her mirror that morning a full twenty minutes. She even chose a dark blue T-shirt instead of her favorite lime green one, because she thought the darker color looked more sincere.

She distracted Dorcas with some extra feed so she could sneak off the back way without the hen following her. When she got to Bea's house (she still couldn't get used to calling it Mr. Rolls' house), she didn't go around to the side entrance, figuring that this sort of meeting deserved the formality of a front door.

"What do you want?" were the words that greeted her as the door opened. A screen door separated her from a sullen-looking Saul.

"Can I come in?" Ruth asked. She had no intention of performing her very impassioned apology on the front porch, which was in the direct line of sight of Mrs. Gorgonzola whenever she sat in her bentwood rocker by her front window.

Saul opened the screen door, stepped back, and gestured into the house with a sweep of his arm.

She heard voices and craned her neck to see if they were coming from the kitchen. She didn't need an audience of neighbors, either.

"Is someone here?"

"Mr. Weeks is outside helping Dad with the garden."

"Oh. Well, in that case," she paused, taking a deep breath to steady herself, "I'm here to give you an apology." She opened her mouth to launch into her speech.

"Don't bother."

"But, I need to bother. I have it all prepared."

"I don't need to hear it." Saul's face was closed and blank. It was like he had disappeared inside himself.

Ruth wasn't called as stubborn as a cat at bath time for nothing. She owed him an apology, she had practiced her apology, and by gum he was going to get an apology. "I know sometimes I can be ..."

Just then the screen door opened and Mr. Rolls and Mr. Weeks came in.

"Well, now, what's this?" Mr. Weeks said, looking from Saul to Ruth and back again. "Two friends hanging out? Off to have some adventures?"

"She's not my friend," Saul said, his face still expressionless. "She was just letting me know what supplies we need for school in September." Saul looked at Ruth. "Thanks for the info. Maybe just email me the list."

Ruth could feel her face flush as all three of them stared at her. Where was her invisibility when she really needed it? Why couldn't the floor open up and swallow her whole, she wondered, because this couldn't possibly be worse.

"Halloooooo!"

Oh yes it could.

Mrs. Gorgonzola stood on the porch peering in through the screen door. "I just wanted to pop over with some ... popovers," she said, giving a little giggle at her own joke and holding up a muffin tray with a towel over the top. Ruth tried not to roll her eyes. Word around Pinkerton was that Mrs. Gorgonzola kept batches of pastries in her freezer so she would have an excuse to poke her nose in any gathering at a moment's notice.

"So, what is this little get-together?" she asked, having the audacity to open the screen door and waltz in without being invited.

Without a word, Saul turned and went upstairs. Ruth

pushed past them and bolted out the door almost knocking the muffin tray out of Mrs. Gorgonzola's hands.

"WELL!" Mrs. Gorgonzola exclaimed.

Ruth did her best to not break into a run as she headed home, knowing from the prickles up the back of her neck that they were watching her go. Dorcas met her at the end of her driveway clucking in annoyance. Ruth scooped her up her in arms.

"I know, I know. I should have brought you along. *That* would have fixed nosy Mrs. Gorgonzola," she told the hen. It was known around the village that Mrs. Gorgonzola was terrified of poultry. Harriet Ings, who lived next door to her, had to build a fortress for her ducks so they wouldn't accidentally wander onto Mrs. Gorgonzola's property. Word was, on a windy night you could still hear the echoes of Mrs. Gorgonzola's screams from the day six years ago when, among her marigolds, she found one of Harriet Ings' ducklings, which had nipped at her ankles.

Back in her room, Ruth fumed. Gloating over an apology would have been better than refusing one altogether. Her bad opinion of Saul worsened. Ruth resolved to banish Saul from her thoughts and pretend like she had never met him. She wouldn't even look in his direction. She would figure out who murdered Bea on her own.

That night as she climbed into bed, Ruth took out the

gloves from her night table drawer. Yellowed and frayed, they looked like someone had picked them out of a dumpster. Maybe the clue was that someone famous wore them? Ruth turned them over in her hands. It struck her then that the gloves were not a matched pair — the pattern of embroidery was different on each one. Was this some sort of fashion statement from long ago? Or were the gloves from two different pairs? Ruth put the gloves back in the drawer.

She lay in the darkness trying to untangle the web of things that had happened since Bea was murdered. None of it made sense. What was Bea doing walking along the banks of the river? Everyone knew how slippery and dangerous they were in springtime. No one more than Beatrice Payens, head of the Teeswater River Embankment Rehabilitation Society. She was the one who posted the warnings each spring on the community bulletin board in the Gas 'n' Go when the Teeswater River began to swell with the melt. Was she running away from someone and slipped? Or did someone drag her there and push her over into the water? But then wouldn't there have been drag marks or signs of a struggle? Mr. Weeks said he saw her walking alone. Calmly. Maybe she was poisoned or drugged and was too confused to know where she was going?

Ruth's thoughts were interrupted by a ping on her bedroom window. Then another. Then another. She went to the window, pulling and then letting go of the vinyl window shade so it snapped up into a roll. She peered out. There was someone in the backyard. Ruth could just make out a silhouette and some movement. She felt safe enough on the second floor to open the window and call, "Hey. Who's out there?"

The figure moved closer to the house, so the light coming from the TV in the den downstairs illuminated their face. It was Saul.

"What do *you* want?" she asked.

"I need to talk to you," he said in a low voice.

"So talk."

"No. Down here. In private."

"Hey, how did you know this was my room?"

"It was the only window with butterfly stickers on it."

Ruth sighed and closed the window. She didn't want to go; she was still furious at him for what happened that afternoon. She could just ignore him, and leave him standing out there, but she had to admit that she was curious about what he had to say for himself. Maybe he was going to apologize to her for not letting her apologize to him? She grabbed her housecoat and went downstairs. There was no way of sneaking past her parents as the den had a view of both the front door and the kitchen, which led to the back door.

"Ruth? Why are you out of bed? Are you dizzy again?" her mother asked, her face crinkling into worry.

"No. I'm fine. I just, um, think I forgot to latch the chicken coop. I'll just be a minute."

Like everyone else in Pinkerton, her parents thought it was perfectly safe to go outside at night. And they would have been right, if there hadn't been a murder in town. But of course, they didn't know that yet. So her mother waved her on and her father never even took his eyes off the screen.

Just outside the back door Ruth stopped to let her eyes adjust to the dark. The back light had been knocked out by a badly aimed soccer ball at least two years earlier and never fixed. She wrapped her housecoat closer around her.

"Thanks for coming out. I wasn't sure you would," Saul said.

"Well, I wasn't sure I would, either," she admitted, then paused, waiting for his apology. When he didn't speak, she said, "Sooo, what is it you couldn't tell me from the window?" Maybe he just needed a little encouragement to apologize.

"Don't come around to Aunt Bea's house anymore."

Ruth was dumbstruck. If it hadn't been so dark out, Saul would have seen her mouth opening and closing like a beached fish, which was just as well, because it was not an attractive look.

"You came all the way over here to tell me you don't ever want to see me again?!" Ruth said, her voice rising slightly. "Don't worry. It's *not* going to be a problem." As if she needed *him* for a friend! Well, he was about to get a piece of her mind and it was going to be a large helping.

"Good," Saul said. "It might be dangerous and I don't want you to get hurt."

That stopped Ruth's tirade in its tracks. What did he say? He didn't want her to get hurt? How would she get hurt going over to Bea's house?

"What do you mean?"

Saul stepped closer. He lowered his voice. "I had to pretend we weren't friends for your own safety. I found an unfinished letter for me in Aunt Bea's journal."

"What did it say?"

"That she was afraid that once she was out of the way, you would become the next target. I'm supposed to ... protect you. If you keep coming around to the house, someone might figure your connection to Aunt Bea."

Ruth shivered as if the words had touched a nerve deep inside her. And although she didn't understand how or why, she was sure, beyond a shadow of a doubt, that she was in terrible, terrible danger.

Chapter 7

Ruth and Saul had arranged to meet by the Mornays' chicken coop at dusk to compare notes.

Ruth stifled a yawn. "Sorry," she said.

Saul raised an eyebrow but didn't ask why she was so tired, which was a good thing, because Ruth didn't want to tell him. She was upset that her nightmares had returned with a vengeance. The night before she heard the rushing of water, felt the stiff breeze on her cheeks, and felt her foot slipping on a muddy bank pulling her closer and closer to the icy water. She sat bolt upright in bed, on full alert, ready to scream so someone would rescue her.

Only, as she sat trembling and soaked in sweat, she could see that she was in her room and not on the banks of the Teeswater River. Everything was fine. She was never able to get back to sleep though, worried that she would wake up to her nightmare coming true. She never knew which ones would come alive and which ones would just haunt her sleep.

"Did you talk to Mrs. Gorgonzola?" Ruth asked. Saul hadn't been too eager to accept his mission to find more information about Bea.

"Yeah. Tell me again why I had to do it and not you?"

"She doesn't like me. Never has. And to make it worse, last week Dorcas decided to hide her egg in the hosta plants by the front door of St. Ignatius. Mrs. Gorgonzola stood outside the church in the rain for over half an hour waiting for Dorcas to leave so she could go in. Personally, I think Dorcas was dawdling on purpose because she hasn't cared for Mrs. Gorgonzola since the day she chased Dorcas away from her lilac bush with a Swiffer mop. Anyway, what did she say?"

"She said there weren't any strangers, visitors, hikers, or lost tourists the day Aunt Bea went missing."

No need to double check Mrs. Gorgonzola's statement. She was more vigilant than Crimestoppers, Citizen Patrol, and Neighborhood Watch all rolled into one.

But the news wasn't what they wanted to hear. Ruth and Saul both let the fact sink in that if no one new was in Pinkerton that day, then that must mean the murderer lived among them.

Ruth shivered. Everyone in the village had lived there for years, including Bea. Had someone been lying in wait all that time? Or was it a "crime of passion," like they called it on those TV police shows?

"Did you find out anything more about the picture?" Saul asked her. It had been Ruth's job to research the hair picture.

"Just that human hair art was a 'thing.' People would make jewelry, pictures, and even lace with hair. Some of it was from living people, some of it from dead ones."

"Do you think it could be the killer's hair? Maybe Aunt Bea was leaving us some evidence to convict them?"

"Then why wouldn't the killer take or destroy the picture after committing the murder?"

"Unless they didn't know she had it?"

"Maybe" Ruth said, not convinced. She swatted at a mosquito whining in her ear. "Ugh, I'm getting eaten alive. Are you sure we can't meet at your house?"

"The farther away from there you are, the safer it is for you."

"I don't even know *why* I'm in danger. It sounds ridiculous to think I'm on someone's hit list just for being friends with Bea."

"I think it's more than that. Did she ever give you anything? Something special? For a birthday or Christmas?"

Ruth shook her head. "Bea didn't like giving 'things' at all. She told me she preferred to give 'experiences.' So for Christmas or my birthday she would buy us tickets to the theater, or an exhibit, or a concert. Stuff like that." Ruth paused to think. "In fact, those three items she asked you to give me were the first 'things' she ever did. Why?"

"Because someone has been searching our house."

Ruth gasped. "Who? Did you catch them?"

"No. I've never seen them do it."

"Then how do you know?" She tilted her head to one side. "You're not one of those conspiracy nuts who wears foil hats on your head and thinks twenty-dollar bills have microphones in them, are you?"

"No, I'm one of those nuts with the eidetic memory who knows where everything was in their room when they leave to go to the lumber store in Beamsville with their dad."

"Maybe you just thought you left things a certain way? Or the wind blew things around?"

"Three different times? And wind doesn't flip books over or move the hangers on the rail in your closet when the doors are closed."

Ruth was too polite to tell Saul that she thought he sounded exactly like those nuts with foil hats. "You think Bea was killed for something she owned, and they're still looking for it?"

Saul nodded.

"What if it's one of the items she gave me?" Ruth asked.

"I don't think she would put your life in danger by giving you the very thing someone would kill to have."

"No. I don't think so either," Ruth said, a sudden wave of

missing her friend washing over her. "What would they be looking for?"

"I don't know. But we need to find out. If we can understand why Aunt Bea was a target, maybe we can figure out who did it. So the picture is a mystery and the gloves are mismatched. What about the frog?"

"I haven't looked at it since you gave it to me. It's in the potting shed."

They stumbled their way in the growing darkness to the corner of the yard. The shed was under a massive oak tree and pitch-black inside. Saul used the light on his cellphone to locate the metal frog sprinkler on a shelf between a broken clay pot and a basket of open seed packets.

Ruth and Saul headed back to the backyard where it was a little less claustrophobic. Saul held his phone light while Ruth inspected the little metal sculpture. The green coating had worn off in spots and the black paint on one of the eyes was half gone, making it look like the frog was winking at her. The hose attachment on its butt had a bit of rust, but other than that, it was pretty solid.

"It's just a sprinkler," Ruth said, giving it to Saul. He handed her the cellphone and she held the light while he had a closer look. He fiddled with the hose attachment.

"Look, it's a bit loose."

He wiggled the end, then twisted it slightly to the left and pulled. The bottom of the frog popped open and something fell out onto the dark ground. They both scrambled to find whatever it was in the grass with only the light from the cellphone.

"Ow! Found it," Ruth said, rubbing the bottom of her bare foot. She grabbed blindly where she had been standing and her hand closed on a small, cold, metal object. She pulled it up into the light.

"It's a key!" she said. The brass was tarnished and the end was worn as if it had been used a lot. The bow of the key looked like a three-leaf clover and had a long, thin chain through it. "You didn't happen to see a pirate chest in Bea's attic, did you?"

"Not so far," Saul said. "But I really don't think Aunt Bea would hide a key to a something you could open with a sledgehammer. It has to be for something else." He held it out to her. "Here. Aunt Bea wanted you to have it. We'll have to figure out what it opens tomorrow. Dad will be wondering where I am."

Ruth exchanged his cellphone for the key and headed inside. She was trying to decide whether or not to tell Saul that she knew exactly what this key unlocked.

⁓ Chapter 8 ⁓

One Saturday afternoon about seven months before Bea died, Ruth had gone over to her house. She was hoping Bea would help her with a history project for school. Ruth was supposed to make a family tree and while her mother knew her grandparents and great-grandparents names back four generations, her father offered very little about his family and had no family records. Ruth knew that Bea had written a whole history of the early settlers of Pinkerton and would know where to look online for some answers.

That day, very uncharacteristically, Bea didn't answer the side door when Ruth knocked. Ruth pushed on the door and it swung open.

"Hi Bea!" Ruth called but heard no answer. She saw the door to the basement open and the light on. A chill went through her wondering if maybe Bea had fallen down the stairs and now lay unconscious at the bottom. She hurried down, her heart beating wildly in her chest. Turned out,

Bea wasn't lying in a heap on the floor; she was in the process of rolling her metal canning shelf back against the wall in front of what looked like to Ruth, from the quick glimpse she got, an old wooden door. Then Bea slipped a key on a chain around her neck under her sweater as she turned around. She was startled to see Ruth standing there.

"I'm so sorry, Bea," Ruth had said breathlessly. "But you didn't answer when I knocked and the basement door was open and I thought …"

Bea held up her hand. "No harm done, Ruth. How nice to know that someone would come to my rescue if I were in trouble." Then Bea led her back upstairs where they had tea and strawberry shortcake. Ruth never did dare ask what the door was or where it led as she got the distinct impression from the shelf hiding it that it was meant to be a secret. She also forgot to ask Bea to help her with her history project. But she never forgot the key on the necklace that Bea wore around her neck.

Ruth fingered the key necklace now hanging around her own neck. She was hesitant to tell Saul what she knew and what she had seen. After all, if Bea had wanted him to know about the door, then wouldn't she have told him in a letter? Or given *him* the key? On the other hand, Ruth argued with herself, Bea had trusted Saul, so she should too. But somehow it was instinctive to her to hold a secret close.

She would have to wait until tomorrow night's meeting at the chicken coop to tell him anyway because tonight Saul had cello lessons in Beamsville. It didn't take much imagination on Ruth's part to realize that tonight would be the perfect opportunity to sneak over to Bea's house to investigate the locked door in the basement by herself while Saul and his dad were out.

After supper Ruth went outside and climbed her maple tree. She could see that Mr. Rolls' car was already gone. She wasn't sure how long cello lessons lasted, but she knew she would have to get moving. As she began to climb down, movement across the road in the back field behind the Gas 'n' Go caught her eye. Someone was creeping around in the bushes that flanked Spencer Creek, which emptied into the Teeswater River. Ruth saw a straw hat bobbing up and down between the branches every now and then. Bea's straw hat.

Was this some kind of trick? Bea was dead, wasn't she? Or maybe, did Bea escape her fate and was letting everyone think she was dead so she could flush out the attacker? Her heart in her throat, Ruth slid down out of the tree. Barely stopping to breathe, she sprinted across the road, cut through the parking lot behind the church, and headed for the creek. She stopped only once to relocate Bea's straw hat, and then took off, wheezing for air.

"Bea? Bea?" she whispered, parting the thick bushes with her hands. A face popped up from behind the leaves right in front of her. The shock of it made her fall backwards into a cedar bush.

It was Harriet Ings. "Oh, Ruth. I didn't see you there."

"What … what are you doing in Bea's hat?" Ruth sputtered out, utterly crushed that it wasn't her friend.

Harriet reached a hand up to touch the hat. "But, this is mine."

Ruth took a closer look and could see that there were plastic chrysanthemums and daisies decorating the hatband. Bea's had had lilies and roses. "Oh. I'm sorry. It looked just like Bea's hat."

"Oh, I know," Harriet Ings said. "That's because I made it for her. I can make you one too, if you like?" Mrs. Ings' face lit up.

"Uh, no. Thanks. I already have a hat."

Mrs. Ings' face fell. "Well then maybe you could help me find Portia?"

Portia was Harriet Ings' pet pig. Ruth wondered if Mrs. Ings knew that most people in town, coming from farming families, thought Portia should end up on a spit at the Thanksgiving Fall Fair. Ruth had watched from her maple tree as practically every last person in the village secretly fed Portia treats to fatten her up. Portia could be anywhere right now, chowing down on some snickerdoodles or pickled beets. Mr. Weeks once fed Portia some crispy bacon, which horrified Ruth because that was basically cannibalism. Portia also didn't realize that Mr. Parker, the farmer down the road who was on the Fall Fair committee, was estimating her weight every time she strolled by.

"I think I saw her by the Gas 'n' Go," Ruth lied. She realized that she was running out of time if she was going to investigate that door and that Portia would make her way home when she was full.

"Why would she be there?" Mrs. Ings asked.

"Swedish meatballs," Ruth said, getting up from the cedar bush and starting to run back across the field leaving behind a very bewildered Mrs. Ings.

Ruth climbed up the maple tree for a look. The lights were on in Bea's house and Mr. Rolls' car was back in the driveway. Portia's insatiable appetite had cost Ruth her chance to find out what Bea was hiding behind that door and if Portia thought she was ever getting another roasted chestnut from Ruth, she was sadly mistaken.

❧ Chapter 9 ❧

Saul was bedridden with bronchitis and Ruth was left alone for days with her own overactive imagination.

That was never a thing.

Ruth was plagued all day with the feeling that someone was watching her and plotting to throw her in the Teeswater River to drown and all night with nightmares that were even worse.

Her dream the night before was one of the ones that felt so real that it took her a few minutes in the morning to convince herself she had been asleep. She had spent the night being chased all around a settlement she thought was Pinkerton, only it didn't really look like Pinkerton — only a few houses lined the main road and the bridge was narrow and made of huge wooden logs. As she ran, her legs felt heavier and heavier. Her route took her along Spencer Creek and across the hayfields behind Bea's house to a dirt road that led to a white clapboard church with a tall steeple that she didn't recognize. With footsteps still bearing down on her, she ran into the woods behind this church and found herself hopelessly stuck in the mud of a bog. She pulled desperately at her legs, trying to dislodge them from the goo and hearing the pounding of the person chasing her getting closer and closer. She couldn't breathe, certain that now she would be caught.

That's when she woke up, panicked and exhausted, the smell of stagnant water and rotting plants still in her nostrils. She could have sworn she had really been there, but she was in her bed, warm and dry.

The smell stayed with her all through breakfast, making her stomach roll as her mother set a bowl of oatmeal in front of her.

"What did you put in that?" Ruth asked, wondering if the smell was actually just the oatmeal.

"Apples and brown sugar," her mother said, giving Ruth a strange look. "Are you feeling okay?"

"Yeah, I'm fine," Ruth said.

"Then why are you sweating?" Her mother put the back of her hand on Ruth's forehead. "Clammy but not feverish."

"I just need some fresh air," Ruth said. "Do you need anything at Sam's?" Ruth wasn't just offering to run to the store to be helpful; she knew that today was bread day. Every Tuesday, Silva's bakery delivered freshly baked buns, breads, and rolls. The smell filled the store and drove out the smell of oil and rubber one day a week. It was just what Ruth needed to cancel out the *Essence de Bog* that didn't seem to want to go away.

"I could use some more brown sugar," her mother said. "And pick up some cold and sinus pills, just in case."

"I'm not sick," Ruth muttered, heading out the door. She walked slowly, breathing deeply, but it was still there. Why wouldn't that stench go away?

The aisles were so crowded in Sam's that Ruth had to turn sideways to squeeze past Mrs. Gorgonzola in the baking section. She was picking out a bag of golden raisins. Ruth shuddered. She hated raisins and had refused to eat them since the day they moved the horsehair sofa to retrieve the remote control that had fallen behind it and found several shriveled green grapes that their cat, Molly, had chased under there. After that, Ruth could only picture factories that were wall to wall with couches with grapes underneath them in the dust slowly shriveling up to raisins. She always picked them out of the apple strudels Mrs. Gorgonzola would bring over whenever she had gossip to share.

"Is there a storm warning nobody told me about?" a voice whispered behind her. Ruth spun around. It was Saul. "I've never seen so many people in here."

"Bread smell," Ruth said giving a quick glance around to

make sure no one was watching them. Who knew that just being friends with someone could put a target on your back.

"Bread smell?" Saul repeated, his eyebrows raising.

"Mrs. Ings always says that sales go up ten percent on bread days."

Saul gave a quick look around the store to see who might be close enough to hear. "Tonight? The coop?"

Ruth nodded. She waited until Saul paid for some cheese slices and a tub of margarine and left before she headed up to the register with the bag of sugar. It was unusual not to see Harriet Ings behind the counter.

"Is Mrs. Ings away?" Ruth asked Sam.

"She's sick, according to Mrs. Gorgonzola, who found a note slipped under her door. Haven't heard from Harriet myself. Hope she's back soon … I've got a shipment to unload."

Ruth paid him and left. But something about Mrs. Ings absence bothered Ruth.

"It's creepy," Ruth told Saul that night at the coop, filling him in on what had happened. "No one has seen Harriet Ings in days."

"What was she doing along Spencer Creek?" Saul asked.

"She said she was looking for Portia."

"You sound like you don't believe her."

"It just seems odd that she was wearing the same thing Bea was, along the banks of a waterway like Bea was, and now she's disappeared, like Bea did."

"Coincidence?"

Ruth shrugged. "Maybe. Maybe I'm reading more into this because I'm tired."

"Do you have a sore throat? Chills? Does it hurt to breathe? Here, I still have some zinc lozenges in my pocket." Saul dug around frantically in his jacket.

"I don't have bronchitis," Ruth said. "I'm just not sleeping very well."

"Dreams?"

"Yeah. Bad ones."

"Bea always said that dreams were a glimpse into the universe," Saul said.

"I sure hope not," Ruth said. "The one last night was awful, and I'd hate to think that that was what the universe was like."

"Maybe it means something."

"Well, I *was* being chased all around Pinkerton. Maybe it's a warning."

"Where did you go in the dream?"

"I started here …" Ruth took a stick and made an X in the dirt where the chickens had scratched the grass away. Then she drew the bridge and the creek and then swooped the line up to the field behind Bea's house, then the curl as she ran into the forest behind the church.

After she finished, she and Saul looked at the lines twisting and bending. It didn't look like Pinkerton's roads at all, but she had a terrible feeling that she was supposed to remember something.

"Does this look familiar to you?" she asked Saul.

Saul moved around to the side of it for a closer look. "Nope. Looks like we're right back at square one. We don't know what anything means."

Ruth took a deep breath. It was time to come clean. "Well, maybe one thing. I think I know what the key might be for."

Saul looked up in surprise. "Really? What?"

"It's just a hunch. Can we look at something in Bea's basement without your dad knowing about it?"

"Why can't my dad know?"

"It seems Bea had secrets, and up until now she had kept them from everyone, including me."

"But Bea is gone now. And we're supposed to figure things out, aren't we?"

Deep down inside Ruth, something stirred. A knowing of sorts.

"I don't think the secrets are meant to be exposed," she said. "I think it's up to me to find and keep them now."

Chapter 10

"What are you doing down there?" Saul asked, ducking his head under the arched concrete bridge that spanned Spencer Creek.

"Uh, looking for Dorcas," Ruth replied, glancing around.

"She's in your driveway."

"Oh."

When she didn't move, Saul crouched down and scooched over to join her. "What are you *really* doing?"

"Hiding from Emily Parsons."

"Why?"

"She's tedious."

Saul nodded as if this needed no further explanation.

Ruth was happy that her mother had let it slip that Emily was back from music camp and home for two weeks before leaving for theater camp. It gave Ruth the chance to avoid her. Emily was convinced that she and Ruth were best friends. Ruth was convinced that if she had to listen to one more minute of Emily detailing every post she read online and then explaining how she felt about it, Ruth's head was going to explode. She had spotted Emily heading to her house as she was coming back from a snack run at Sam's and had ducked under the bridge. Squatting under a bridge getting damp shoes seemed like a small price to pay to prevent a brain explosion.

"I think we might have a chance to explore the basement," Saul said. "Dad has a meeting tonight in Hanover. With travel time, I figure we'd have about two hours."

Ruth nodded. "Have you been down there yet?"

"Nope."

While Ruth was glad he wasn't poking around and discovering things without her, she was surprised. If it were her, she knew there was no way she would have been able to resist going down there before now.

"What time should I come?"

"Dad's probably leaving around 6, so maybe 6:15?"

"I'll be there."

"Right. I'd better go. It'll be pretty difficult to keep up the pretense that we're not friends if we're seen down under this bridge together."

Saul put a hand down on the ground in order to shift his weight from a crouch to start moving out. That's when Ruth heard a blood-curdling scream. It had come from Saul.

He jumped back, banging his head on the edge of a metal construction plate bolted to the bridge support.

"Was that a worm? It was a worm, wasn't it? Did you see it?" He was frantically wiping one palm on his pants while rubbing his head with the other.

He was hyperventilating. Ruth peered at the mud where his hand had been. The tail of a juicy, fat earthworm just disappeared down a hole.

"Nope, just some mud," she said.

Saul's breathing started to slow. He looked back at the ground. "Oh, sorry. I thought it was a worm."

Ruth said nothing. This wasn't the first time she had to deal with someone's phobia. After all, she had been the one who found Mrs. Gorgonzola last May trapped under the picnic table behind Sam's Gas 'n' Go where she was screaming hysterically. Apparently, she had been heading home when a wild turkey had swooped down just missing her head as it tried to pick a fight with Portia for the container of strawberries that had fallen off the delivery truck.

Mrs. Gorgonzola hadn't ventured out of her house for nineteen days after the incident, worried that the turkey was still lurking around. She was forced to serve Mr. Gorgonzola all her elaborate frozen casseroles and pastries saved for 'fact-finding missions,' because she couldn't bring herself to go to Sam's for fresh supplies. Mr. Gorgonzola seemed happy with the turn of events — he hadn't had Chicken Diane in almost fifteen years. Some said they had seen him at dusk scattering corn kernels around their property to lure the wild turkey back.

Saul duckwalked out from under the bridge, still rubbing his head, had a quick look around and then scrambled up the bank back toward Bea's house.

Ruth waited under the bridge a while longer, hoping that Emily had given up waiting for her and gone home again. She peeked out and, seeing the coast clear, made a run for her maple tree. She knew she was going to get a lecture from her mother when she went back inside. Her mother never really understood why Ruth preferred hanging around with an elderly lady rather than girls her own age. Ruth struggled to explain that Bea made her feel like what she had to say was important. And interesting. And worth listening to. The opposite of invisible. The opposite of Emily Parsons.

Ruth sat among the leaves, her sadness at missing her friend battling with anger at whoever did this to her. What secret could Bea have been hiding that was worth being killed over? And why was she sure Ruth could figure it out? Ruth didn't consider herself super smart, which was proven by the fact that so far, she had no idea what the three weird items were supposed to mean. Sure, they had found a key to a door, but even the door wasn't really *that* hard to find, if you were looking. And the key itself? Well, even online you could look up videos on how to pick locks.

"Emily waited for over an hour for you," Ruth's mother admonished her as she finally came in for supper. "Where were you?"

Ruth had never disclosed her tree perch to anyone in her family. She knew that the minute they found out, she wouldn't get any peace there.

"I was just down by the creek, uh, I thought I saw Portia."

"Is that pig running wild again? I had better not find her in my garden," her mother said. "The last time she destroyed three rows of beets in under an hour. If it happens again, I'm coming after her with a roasting pan."

Ruth was relieved that Portia had diverted her mother's attention from Emily. She lucked out over dinner, too, when her brother George announced that Captain Picard of the nineties Star Trek series was way better than Captain Kirk of the original Star Trek series. Chaos ensued when her father snorted in derision telling George that Captain Kirk would never have allowed Wolf 359 to happen and George countered with the fact that Kirk cheated on the Kobayashi Maru test. As voices got louder and opinions got more entrenched, Ruth used her invisibility to slip away from the table without so much as a blip in the argument. It was already six thirty. Ruth hated being late. Instead of taking the longer, more hidden route through the woods, she decided to head up the main road.

She was just about to cross over in front of Bea's house when Mr. Weeks came by on his bicycle, slowed and stopped. She startled because she hadn't heard him coming.

"I don't think they're home," he said, nodding in the direction of Bea's house. "I saw the car pull out a little while ago."

"Oh, I wasn't going there," Ruth lied. "I'm looking for Dorcas."

Mr. Weeks laughed and started off again. "That chicken's got wandering feet. Good luck."

Ruth pretended to poke around the grassy ditches on the sides of the road until the bicycle rounded the corner and was out of sight before scooting up Bea's driveway, knocking on the side door and slipping inside.

"You're late," Saul said.

"Well, I had to duck out of a heated Star Trek argument that almost came to blows and then dodge a nosy neighbor practically running me down on their bike."

"Sounds hazardous," he said, leading the way down the stairs into the basement. "So where is the door?"

"Here, help me roll these shelves out of the way." Ruth and Saul yanked and pushed until finally the heavy metal shelves began to move on their metal wheels. They pulled it out away from the wall and then to the side. Behind it was a door with a flat front, painted gray to blend in with the cement blocks that made up the house foundation. In fact, unless you knew to look there, you would never really notice it behind the shelving unit full of mason jars.

Ruth pulled out the key necklace, ready to unlock the door, but before she could slip the chain over her head, Saul pulled on the door and it started swinging open.

"You mean it wasn't even locked?" Ruth said.

"Nope, and look, the lock is huge. That can't possibly be the key."

The lock was at least three times the size of the key. Ruth was confused. She had clearly seen Bea putting the key away just outside the door. If it wasn't for the door, what could it be for?

Inside the opening, the air was damp and musty. Ruth pulled out the LED flashlight she had remembered to throw in her pocket and shone it into the blackness. The light barely reached the back wall which was just rock and dirt. Ruth walked in for a closer look. Saul came in behind her shining his phone light.

The room was larger than they expected and then Ruth saw something she didn't expect in the back left corner.

"Over here, Saul. Quick!" she called.

And that's when they heard it — the creak of the heavy door moving and the clunk of the latch closing behind them, locking them in. Ruth ran back and pushed. The door wouldn't budge. She and Saul both tried together. She looked through the keyhole, but the basement was dark. She spun her flashlight beam around to Saul and saw what she was feeling reflected on his face: Panic.

Chapter 11

They tried again to push the door open, but it was no use.

"How much air do you think we have?" Saul asked, a catch in his voice.

"Plenty."

"You're just saying that, aren't you?"

"No. Can't you feel it? There's a breeze." Ruth shone her flashlight back in the corner. "Look, there's a crawlspace down at the bottom of the wall. That's what I was going to show you when the door closed."

Ruth walked over and knelt down to shine her light into the hole.

"How far back does it go?" Saul asked.

"I can't see the end."

Ruth crawled forward on the cold stone floor through the small opening, brushing some cobwebs out of the way. Once through the wall, the ground turned to dirt, but the ceiling was higher again and allowed her to stand up. She heard Saul scrabbling through behind her. They shone their lights all around the space. The walls were stone, the ceiling, wooden beams, and the floor, packed dirt.

And it wasn't a room at all — it was a tunnel.

"Where does it go?" Saul asked.

"There's only one way to find out," Ruth said, starting to walk towards the yawning black hole in front of her. "Which way do you think we're going?" she asked, trying to work out which way they were heading above ground.

Saul fiddled with his phone. "Got a compass here."

He tapped it a few times and then spun a little, watching the dial on his screen. "Northwest."

Ruth tried to work out which way Bea's house was pointing, so she could imagine what was northwest of it.

"What's behind Bea's house?"

"Just fields and woods, I think. Do you think maybe this is a mining tunnel?"

"No, I don't think so. The walls wouldn't be this smooth, they would be jagged."

"Then what is it?"

"A passageway," Ruth said, not sure herself why she was so certain of that statement.

They continued on in the darkness that was only held back by their lights for what seemed like miles. The air was musty and damp. As they went on, the passage got narrower and the ceiling lower, the air stuffier. Ruth wondered if they had walked all the way to Beamsville underground.

"Are we still going northwest?" Ruth asked.

"More west than north now. Where do you think it leads?"

"Nowhere," Ruth said, stopping suddenly.

"Well, no one would build a tunnel like this if it went nowh…"

He stopped as they both stood before a wall of stone and dirt blocking the way. It was a dead end.

"Was someone just pulling a prank building this?" He huffed. "To see how many dumb people would walk to the end of it?"

"I don't think so. I think this is a cave-in. Look, the tunnel continues past where the rubble is." Ruth pulled at the loose dirt near the wall.

"So we really *are* trapped. We can't get out the way we came in, and we can't get out the way we are going."

"I can still feel air moving, though," Ruth said. She walked to the other side of the tunnel and held up her hand. "See, over here. I think the roof has collapsed a bit. I can see some light shining through the gap between the old beams."

She scrabbled up the pile of rubble and began clawing away at a small hole at the top. Saul joined her. Slowly, the hole widened and Ruth caught a glimpse of the sky.

"Keep digging!" Ruth encouraged as Saul panted.

The hole was finally large enough for Ruth to try and squeeze through. She got stuck around her hips for a few moments, which resulted in having Saul's hands on her butt, pushing — an embarrassing interlude that they both deliberately never mentioned again. After she got out and helped pull Saul through the hole, they had a good look around.

They were in a small clearing surrounded by trees. The ground was uneven and rose to a bit of a mound in the middle of the space. Ruth sat on a protruding rock and took a few deep breaths. She didn't want to admit to Saul that she had been very close to a panic attack. Saul, for his part, didn't want to admit to Ruth that he was more worried about finding worms in the dirt they were moving than he was about running out of air.

"Where are we?" Saul asked.

"Hard to say here in the woods. Maybe if we climb a tree, we can see a building or something," she said.

"You mean, maybe if *you* climb a tree …"

Ruth sighed. "Fine. I'll see what I can see up there; you see what you can see down here. I mean, that tunnel had to be heading *somewhere*."

Ruth found an oak tree and began making her way from branch to branch going higher and higher until she reached the point where her weight was making the tree sway somewhat every time she moved. She parted the branches to get a better look, but she wasn't totally above the tree line. But there was something in the distance that might help.

"I think I've found something!" they both said in unison.

Ruth carefully climbed down out of the tree. "I know where we are," she said.

"And I know where the tunnel was going," Saul said. "But, you first."

Ruth pointed past Saul. "I managed to see the spire of St. Ignatius. If we walk in that direction, we'll get back to Pinkerton. So, where was the tunnel going?"

"Right here."

"Here? A clearing in the forest? For what? Was Bea a closet Druid and wanted easy access to a tree-hugging ceremony?" Ruth deliberately pushed away memories of Mrs. Gorgonzola's whispers about Bea's secret past of cults and buried treasure. Although, if she allowed herself to admit it, those theories were seeming less far-fetched with every passing day.

"Don't think it was Druids … whoever came here, wanted access to a building."

Saul was right. As they cleared away some of the weeds, Ruth could see that the mound was the remains of stone walls.

"What do you think this was?" Ruth asked.

"Can't tell from a hill of rubble," Saul said. "But there must be a record of it somewhere."

"Yes, of course there is," Ruth murmured. She looked at Saul. "The answer is in your living room."

"I don't think …"

"It will be in a book that Bea wrote," Ruth said. "A whole history of Pinkerton. It's on the bookcase by the window. She showed it to me once, but I wasn't really interested at the time. It's funny, I remember her smiling as she put it back. She mumbled something like, 'There may come a time when you are *very* interested.'"

"Well, I'm interested now," Saul said. "We'd better get back. It's getting dark and my dad will be home soon."

Ruth and Saul picked their way through the forest in the direction of the spire until they came out of the trees into a big hayfield behind Bea's house.

"Oh no, my dad's back already. I've gotta run," Saul said sprinting off.

Ruth skirted the hayfield and slipped across the road and into the woods behind her house.

She never noticed that someone was watching them.

Chapter 12

"Miller's Farm?" Ruth whispered, in case her brothers were around, playing hide and seek in the gloom of the backyard at sunset. "Are you sure that's what we found?"

"I think the stone foundation might be a pig barn," Saul said, opening the book he brought and showing her the image of an old agricultural building. "It's not really clear in the book where it was exactly, but it says there was a farm back there long ago."

"A tunnel to a pig barn?" Ruth searched her memory. "That makes no sense at all. And anyway, I think the old farm was on the other side of Highway 27. There was an old stone silo that fell down after the big storm about six years ago."

Saul took a stick and drew in the dirt. "In the book it sounds like the farm was here." He made a square to signify Bea's house and put an X behind it for the farm.

Ruth took the stick from him and erased his drawing. She made her own marks on the ground. "No, look, the road goes over the bridge and past Bea's house here and bends that way. The farm is over here, but the ruins were over there. We walked this way back to town, remember?" She drew their route, stepped back and pointed. And then it finally hit her. She knew what she was supposed to see. She dropped the stick and ran into the house, leaving behind a bewildered Saul standing in the shadows. When she came back, she was out of breath, half from running up to her bedroom and back, and half from excitement.

"I … huh, huh … found something." She thrust the old yellowed gloves at Saul. He turned them over but looked at her questioningly.

"Look at the pattern," Ruth said. "Now look at what I drew on the ground."

Saul shook his head again and held the gloves back out to her.

"The embroidery isn't decoration," Ruth said, pointing to the gloves. "It's a *map*. That's why the two gloves don't match. The map continues from one glove to the other. This marking must be one side of the bridge, and the other side is on the other glove. And this flower here, the rose, for sure that's Bea's house. Roses were one of her favorite flowers."

"The vine here is Highway 27 through town?" Saul asked.

"Right. It continues over here onto the left glove. This design could be wheat, because the farm that had the pigs also had huge wheat fields. And here's the Teeswater River and Spencer Creek winding through it all."

"So the stone foundation would be …"

"Right here," Ruth said, pointing at a small design. Two short lines crossed each other roughly where they had emerged from the underground tunnel. "X marks the spot?"

Saul turned the glove slightly. "Or not an X … maybe a cross?"

"You mean, like a church? Are there any old churches in the book besides St. Ignatius?"

"I think there was." Saul opened the book again and flipped through the pages. "Here. Old Parish Church."

"Not a very descriptive name," Ruth said, taking the book from Saul. "Not a very impressive building, either."

The faded black and white photo in Bea's book showed a small, rectangular stone building. The gable above the wooden front door had a round window inlaid with stained glass. It was possible to see down the right side of the church only slightly because of the angle of the building in the picture, but it looked to Ruth like there were two arched windows. Ruth had a funny feeling she had seen this church before. Bea had probably shown her the picture when she was writing the book.

"Hard to believe a whole church could be reduced to a pile of rubble," Ruth said.

"Wait. So the tunnel led to the Old Parish Church? Bea dug an underground route to church?" Saul asked. "That's all it was?"

Ruth shook her head. "Can't be what she used it for. It says here that the church burned down in 1884."

"How can a church made of stone burn down?"

Ruth sighed. "The inside was all wood, of course. All that would be left after a fire would be four stone walls. They must have collapsed eventually like the silo."

"Why didn't they just rebuild it?"

"The caption here says that the early settlers felt the old church was too small and too far out of town so they built St. Ignatius to replace it."

The sun had almost set, and it was getting too dark to see the pages clearly.

"I'm going to take a better look at the whole book tomorrow," Saul said. "I think there's a clue we've missed."

"What makes you think that?"

"The inscription in the front."

Ruth flipped back to the title page. There, in Bea's very distinctive handwriting, was:

For Saul:
That you might truly understand your new home.
Aunt Bea

"Did you know she left it to you?" Ruth asked.

Saul shook his head. "Not until I opened it."

Ruth had to agree it was an odd inscription. Sure, it was nice to know the history of a place you've moved to, but why did she write "truly understand"? What was there to understand about Pinkerton? Ruth supposed it was the same as any other tiny hamlet that had not enough entertainment and more than enough nosy neighbors.

"We'll meet tomorrow night? Same time, same place?" Saul asked.

"Yup," Ruth said. "You study the book. I need to find out about Harriet Ings. Mom said she was back at work this morning."

"You don't think Mrs. Ings could be a killer, do you?"

Ruth raised her eyebrows. "Have you never watched any murder mystery shows? I may have lived next to these people all my life, but even I don't know what lurks in their minds. People living in places like Pinkerton can only take so many strawberry socials, birding tours, and bingo nights before they snap. Harriet Ings is meek and mild with no enemies. That type always ends up being the killer."

"But why would she target Aunt Bea?"

Ruth shrugged. "Could be something as small as Bea forgetting to set out Mrs. Ings' pear chutney at the last Dressings and Sauces Association meeting. Who knows what tips unstable people over the edge? Then, after the crime, realizing what she did, Harriet Ings made and planted a replica of Bea's straw hat in the rose bush by the river, to make everyone believe she'd fallen in and drowned."

"Where do you think she's been this past week, if she wasn't home sick like she said?"

Ruth gave an exasperated sigh. "Covering up her crime, of course. Bleaching murder weapons to remove traces of blood. Wiping fingerprints from the scene of the crime. That sort of thing."

Saul looked a little shocked, and a lot confused. "Oh. Well, I'd better go."

"Wait a minute," Ruth said. "What about the door in the basement. Why couldn't we open it yesterday?"

"When I got home, I went to check it, but it still wasn't locked and swung open easily. Maybe it was just stuck on something when we tried to push it?"

Ruth nodded, but deep down, she didn't believe it. Something or maybe someone had prevented them from getting out.

Saul opened the potting shed door and turned. "Be careful out there, okay?" Then he slipped out after checking the coast was clear and headed home.

Ruth went inside and up to her room. She lay in bed letting what Saul said sink in. *Be careful out there.* It was the first time since Bea had died that someone had worried about her.

∽ Chapter 13 ∽

That night, Ruth fell into an uneasy sleep plagued with dreams. She was walking up a gravel path. The Old Parish Church was ahead of her, fully restored. The bright sun shone on the front of the building, showing the gleaming colors of the stained-glass window and accentuating the beautiful carvings on the door. People were milling all around her, all in straw hats. Each one had different flowers and ribbons, but every time Ruth thought she had seen Bea and tapped on her shoulder, the person who turned around in the hat wasn't her.

Ruth woke up sad and empty. Breakfast with her six brothers didn't help — it was surprisingly hard to maintain an appetite surrounded by a who-can-shove-the-most-French-toast-in-their-mouth-at-one-time contest. Ruth escaped outside as fast as she could. She blamed the bad timing of her exit on her brothers. Just as she rounded the corner of the house, only steps from the safety and invisibility of her maple tree perch, she ran into Emily Parsons, who apparently wasn't perceptive enough to know that Ruth had been avoiding her.

"Guess who liked my post about our music camp end-of-season performance?" Emily blurted out as soon as Ruth was in earshot.

Of course Ruth didn't know or even care who had liked her post, but Emily seemed to be expecting a response. Out of curiosity, Ruth said nothing, wondering exactly how long Emily would stand there, waiting for an answer. Ruth never did find out because just then, Dorcas wandered up the driveway on her way to hide her egg. Emily stared at Dorcas as if she had never seen a chicken before.

"That hen is loose," Emily said, pointing at Dorcas.

"She's going for her daily walk," Ruth said.

"Shouldn't she be on a leash or something?"

Ruth decided that a stupid question deserved a stupid answer. "We tried, but she kept pulling her head out of the collar. Besides, she hasn't tried to peck anyone's kneecaps in weeks."

Emily paled and took a step back. "I really only came to pick up some eggs for Mrs. Ings. Your mom said yesterday that you had extra this week."

"You've spoken to Mrs. Ings?" Ruth asked. "I heard she was really sick. What's wrong with her?" Would Emily let something slip that would prove her theory that Harriet Ings wasn't really sick but was a criminal mastermind trying to cover her tracks?

"Um, I'm not supposed to gossip," Emily said.

"Yeah, no, me neither." Ruth realized she was going to have to weasel the truth out of Emily. Trouble was, Ruth wasn't that good at trying to trick people into giving her information. She was going to have to channel her inner Nancy Drew.

"When did you speak to her? I haven't seen her in ages."

"Oh, my mom sent me over there to see if I could help."

"I'm surprised Mrs. Ings is eating eggs if she has … high cholesterol?"

"I didn't hear anything about her not eating eggs."

"Oh, I meant chocolate eggs, you know, because of her … diabetes?"

"I didn't know she had diabetes," Emily said, looking concerned.

"No, I guess I mean the chocolate in them, which triggers her … migraine headaches?"

"She didn't mention a pain in her head to me, just the pain in her foot from a really bad attack of gout."

"Right. That's what I meant. Gout. And how worrying about it was giving her headaches," Ruth finished lamely. Well, *that* wasn't what she was expecting.

"I don't think she's that worried," Emily said, heading toward their back door and completely forgetting her instructions not to gossip. "I think she's just got a thing for that podiatrist in Beamsville. She's gone every day for over a week now. If anything, she's hoping the gout won't go away so she can keep going to see him."

Ruth was stunned. Mrs. Ings was crushing on a foot doctor? That's why she was away? Not burying a murder weapon? Or burning blood-splattered clothing? While part of her was relieved that Bea hadn't been betrayed by someone she counted as a friend, Ruth had to face facts. If not Harriet Ings — then who?

ᕦ Chapter 14 ᕤ

"We're back to square one," Ruth told Saul after giving him the story about Harriet Ings and the Passionate Podiatrist. She peeked out the barn door to make sure no one had seen her sneak over to Bea's property. They couldn't meet at the coop later because Saul had his cello lesson. "No suspect. No leads."

"You don't suspect Harriet Ings anymore? Even if she really was ill the last few days, she could have still done it, you know."

"Yeah, but when I think about it, Harriet Ings is so thin that she struggles to walk upright in a strong wind. There's no way she'd be able to overpower Bea. Bea helped with the hay harvest every year and threw bales around like tea towels. She could have fought off someone like Harriet Ings easily."

"And we're a bit weak on motive," Saul added. "A forgotten pear chutney isn't enough to murder someone over."

"Well, maybe not, although you have no idea how seriously those ladies take this stuff. Four years ago at the Fall Fair, Mrs. Parsons — Emily's mom — had to be restrained by committee members when she learned Mrs. Gorgonzola's red pepper jelly had beaten hers. She claimed Mrs. Gorgonzola stole her recipe, which was her grandmother's, and passed it off as her own. Mrs. Gorgonzola said Mrs. Parsons shouldn't flatter herself, that the only thing the Parson red pepper jelly was good for was to oil her furniture."

"I thought the countryside was full of helpful neighbors and smiling farmers."

"If that were true, then Bea would still be here," Ruth said.

They were quiet for a while as they pondered that. Ruth wondered if having a mother like Mrs. Parsons was the reason Emily was so tedious. Maybe she'd have to cut her a little slack when she got back from theater camp.

"Well, who else could it be?" Saul asked. "What about Mrs. Fazarri, the church secretary?"

"Nah, she would have confessed to Father Donatello already."

"Mr. Clarke? The guy who repairs bicycles in his garage?"

Ruth shook her head. "He was on holiday in Madeira at that time."

"Miss Makoti, with the alpaca farm?"

"She was hosting a fiber workshop in her barn with a

bunch of knitting fanatics," Ruth said. "I can't think of who else it could be right now."

"Well, I don't have much new info either," Saul said, pulling out his phone and bringing up a picture of the page from Bea's book with the Old Parish Church on it, "except this."

"You showed that to me yesterday."

"I know. But last night I read the page more closely. It mentions the architect of the church ... a Mr. Thomas Fuller."

"So?"

Saul used two fingers to make the image zoom in. "If you look really closely at the text on the page, it looks like his name was underlined and then erased."

Ruth squinted at the screen. "That's the biggest lead we've got? Erased pencil lines? Well, add it to the pile of useless clues with a key that doesn't open anything and a map to nowhere." She plopped down on a bale of hay. "We are terrible sleuths." She pulled a thin stalk from the bale and chewed on it. "And you should sell this hay, you know. The hayfield will be ready to harvest soon and you'll have more than this barn can hold. Bea always sold it to make a bit of money."

"Who'd she sell it to?"

"She used to sell it to Sam for his goats, but they had a

big argument last year. He said she told him one price, she said she told him another and that he was always trying to cheat her. She told me that he would show up with less cash on him than they'd agreed to, and last year she'd had enough. She said she would rather burn it than sell it to him."

"Was he angry?" Saul asked.

"Of course! Bea had always given him a good deal because he was local. After the argument he had to pay a lot more for hay from a farm outside Beamsville. Told everyone that's why he had to sell his goats — because he couldn't afford to feed them anymore."

"Goats aren't worth a lot of money, though, are they?"

"These weren't just any goats … they were cashmere goats."

"Is that good?" Saul asked.

"Cashmere," Ruth repeated, as if that would clarify things. Who didn't know what cashmere was? Saul apparently. "Like cashmere sweaters?"

"I'll take your word for it," Saul said, clearly wanting to end the conversation before he got a fashion lecture. "That sounds like motive to me."

"Sam?" Ruth had never considered Sam a suspect. Would he kill in a rage over losing his valuable goats? "I guess he would be strong enough after lifting heavy boxes all day. But Sam kill Bea?" Ruth still couldn't quite believe it.

"Well, he had the motive and means. That just leaves opportunity. Where was he the day Bea went missing?"

Ruth called up that day in her memory. She hadn't thought about it in detail since it happened because it hurt to think about it. What if she had gone over to Bea's house that day, like she'd planned? Would that have changed the chain of events? Would Bea still be alive?

Ruth had woken up that Tuesday morning with a headache. It had been raining for three days and although it was still blustery that day, the sky had cleared. Ruth thought about staying home from school. She didn't feel like enduring the noise and bright lights, not to mention her family history project was due and her family tree was still missing a lot of branches. If she stayed home, she could visit Bea and get some help to fill out her project and also be able to rest her aching head.

But at the last minute, Ruth felt a compulsion to get dressed and catch the school bus. It was almost like she was being propelled out of Pinkerton that day. She was uneasy all day, but blamed it on her increasingly painful headache. Almost as soon as she stepped down off the bus after school, she heard about Bea's disappearance. Ruth's knees buckled and she staggered home. Although the search went on for three weeks and Ruth hung on to the hope that Bea would be found all right, deep down she knew that she would never see her friend again.

"As far as I know, Sam was at the store, as usual. Lots of time to slip away while pretending to be working in the back room doing inventory or something," Ruth said.

"A solid suspect then," Saul said. "But how do we prove it?"

"I guess we get him to admit he was angry about the goats and blamed Bea," Ruth said. "And then make sure he doesn't have an alibi for the afternoon when she went missing."

Ruth slipped home and climbed her maple tree to think. Sam may have had the means, motive, and opportunity to harm Bea, but Ruth struggled to imagine that someone she saw almost every day would take revenge in such a savage way.

But then, Ruth didn't know how deep the secrets ran in Pinkerton at all.

⮞ Chapter 15 ⮜

Ruth put a bag of coconut and a bottle of window cleaner on the counter at Sam's. Harriet Ings rang the items in.

"I'm glad you're feeling better," Ruth said as she tapped her mom's debit card on the machine.

"Oh, well, I'm still having twinges of pain now and then," Harriet said quickly. "My gout still needs to be closely monitored."

Ruth smiled and nodded. She noticed Mrs. Ings' straw hat atop her sweater on a stool behind the counter.

"What happened to Bea's straw hat that I found by the river and turned over to the police?" Ruth asked, realizing that she hadn't seen it since then.

"They kept it as evidence. I don't know when or if they'll ever release it."

"Oh."

"I could make one for you," Harriet Ings offered again.

Ruth didn't have the heart to turn her down a second time.

Besides, she had an idea. "Could you make me one exactly like Bea's?" she asked.

"No problem," Harriet Ings said, almost quivering. "I still have all the materials I need. Bea was very particular in how she wanted it to look. I still have the instructions she gave me." She thrust the receipt at Ruth. "It won't take but a day or two. Unless my gout acts up, of course," she said, wincing slightly.

"Thanks," Ruth said. It struck her that if Bea knew she was going to be murdered, maybe she left the hat on the rose bush herself as a clue. If Ruth couldn't have the actual hat, maybe a replica would give her some inspiration.

After dropping off the coconut and glass cleaner for her mom, Ruth snuck off through the woods and across the road to Bea's place. She knew from the strong ammonia smell that the chicken coop needed cleaning out, and that was as good a reason as any to escape for the day. She skirted Bea's house and waded through the hayfield away from the village. Although she didn't have a firm plan in her mind, her feet seemed to be taking her back to the Old Parish Church ruins. Every now and then she stopped and turned expecting to see someone, the feeling of being followed was so strong. But no one was there.

When she got to the woods, she picked her way through the undergrowth until she found the clearing again. She stood there, trying to recall her dream so she could picture the church as it would have been before the fire. She wondered what it all meant. Why would Bea have a tunnel in her basement that went to the ruins of a church?

Her thoughts were interrupted by the sound of someone shuffling through the bushes behind her. She looked around frantically for somewhere to hide, but she didn't have time to run into the woods across the clearing away from the noise, and in the open, she was completely exposed. She would have to turn and face whoever was coming.

Ruth needed a weapon, but there wasn't a single tree branch on the ground and not a bit of scrap metal was left in the rubble. All she could think of was to grab a rock, but even those seemed to be held fast to the ground with vines and roots. The shuffling seemed to stop, which was even more terrifying to Ruth. Where had they gone? She yanked with all her might on a rock and it gave way so suddenly that she fell backwards. The rock went flying into the bush, which started the shuffling again.

She had knocked the wind out of herself and as she lay there, gasping for breath — totally vulnerable — she heard the shuffling coming closer and then stopping. She turned her head to look at her attacker, wondering if Bea's concern about her being the next victim was about to come true.

A big pink snout stared back at her.

Portia.

Ruth rolled over and sat up, her lungs letting in a bit more air so she could stop gasping. Portia bobbed her head a bit and snorted as if she was delighted to see Ruth. Ruth wished she could tell Portia how glad she was to see *her* and not someone else. Portia began rooting around and making happy pig noises.

"Now how did you get so far out of town?" she asked Portia. Portia wiggled her little bum, shaking her tail in answer. Portia wandered over to the oak tree that Ruth had climbed when she was there with Saul and rooted around under it.

"You've been here before, haven't you? You've been feasting on acorns! So, this is where you go when you disappear."

Ruth slowly got to her feet, rubbing her hip, which was sure to have a bruise from where she landed on something sharp. She looked back at the spot to see what it was and caught a glimpse of something glinting in the sun. She bent down and, moving some dirt aside, pulled it out. The sun hit it full on and there was a flash of red.

"It's a brooch!" she said. Portia raised her head, but as it didn't smell like food, went back to foraging.

It was hard to tell whether it was oval- or diamond-shaped because it was so caked with mud and clay. But in the middle was a stone that, when Ruth tilted the brooch slightly to catch the sunlight, glowed a deep blood red.

Her hand closed around the brooch, and she shut her eyes. For less than a heartbeat she heard the whoosh of fabric, the tinkle of crystal, and the hum of a violin string. Then it was gone.

Ruth opened her eyes. She was surprised she was still standing in the clearing because what she had just experienced had been so real, she was sure she had been somewhere else for a moment. It was like one of her vivid dreams … only this time she was awake when she had it.

She looked at the brooch in her hand and wondered how she hadn't seen it the other day when she and Saul had been there. She could see now that when she had fallen, she had landed on the little pile of dirt near the opening they had made from the blocked tunnel. Had the brooch been on the ground or had it been in the dirt from the tunnel? Ruth put the brooch in her pocket and dug around the same spot looking for more items, but she didn't find anything else.

Ruth walked over to where Portia was still snuffling around and heard the crunch of acorns under her shoe. Portia looked up at the sound and then butted Ruth's ankle to move her off her treat. Ruth stepped out of her way. There's no way she would win a head-butting contest with a full-grown sow.

Portia finally finished crunching and was wandering off through the woods heading back home. Ruth did not want to be alone in the clearing and wasn't too proud to follow a pig. The feeling of being watched hadn't entirely left her, and Ruth hoped Portia would be her porcine bodyguard. Ruth had seen the normally mild-mannered Portia revert to her feral DNA whenever anyone dared to challenge her for so much as a Cheezie that had fallen on the ground. It was clear that to Portia, some things were worth fighting for. Ruth hoped that if push came to shove, she would be one of those things, even if she wasn't covered in orange cheddar powder.

❧ Chapter 16 ❧

Portia had taken a very roundabout route into town that took them over to the banks of Teeswater River and around the back of Mrs. Gorgonzola's and Mrs. Ings' properties until they ended up behind Sam's Gas 'n' Go. Portia headed to the dumpster to look for scraps that had missed the bin. Ruth sat on the picnic table under the alder tree in the back, where Mrs. Gorgonzola had taken refuge from the wild turkey, to think.

Portia squealed as she found something delicious to feast on next to the dumpster. At that moment, Sam came barreling out of the store's back door with fire in his eyes, brandishing a melon-slicing knife. Ruth jumped to her feet.

"Get away you filthy pest. I'm tired of slipping on your pig droppings. Take off or I'll slice you in two and throw you in the river!" His voice was raspy and the veins in his neck bulged.

Ruth believed he would do it too. So did Portia, who took off with a squeal back towards Mrs. Ings' property. Ruth was shaken. She had never seen Sam so angry.

"And I'll enjoy doing it!" he yelled after Portia. Then he saw Ruth standing there. He gave what sounded to Ruth like a nervous laugh.

"Didn't see you there," he said, wiping his brow. "Gotta keep the critters in check or they'll run rampant."

Ruth smiled and nodded as if she agreed, but she kept her eyes glued on the melon slicer that was still in his hand.

"Well, gotta go," she said, waving.

"Wait a minute," Sam said, brandishing the knife. "You still go over to Bea's house now and then?"

Ruth paled. Was Sam suspicious that she was involved with whatever secret Bea had been hiding? Had he seen Ruth sneak over to visit Saul? Had she just become the next target of Bea's killer? There was only one thing to do — lie.

"No. Mr. Rolls is actually quite nasty and his son is annoying." It physically hurt her stomach to lie so blatantly. The couple of times she had seen Mr. Rolls he had been so nice and polite to her. And Saul, well, Ruth had to admit he was growing on her.

Sam's eyebrows furrowed. "Really? Hugh seems real gentlemanly to me."

Ruth just shook her head and started to back away again.

"Well, just the same, seeing as you live close to them, could you do me a favor?"

Ruth felt trapped. She certainly didn't want to connect herself with anything to do with Bea, but she wasn't about to anger a man with an eight-inch blade in his hand.

"Sure."

"Young Saul picked up their mail this morning, but he forgot one. It's still in the box. Wondered if you'd drop it off."

Ruth exhaled. The post boxes along the back wall of the store were crammed together in a corner and only lit by a dust-covered bulb. Mail was often missed. While Canada Post might not approve of Sam's solution to send something along with a neighbor, it's how things had always been done in Pinkerton.

"No problem."

"Ask Mrs. Ings for it. She has the key."

Ruth nodded and tried to walk calmly around to the front and not to look behind her to make sure Sam had gone in the back door and wasn't following her with his knife.

"Oh, I was working on your hat on my lunch break," Mrs. Ings said as she handed Ruth the key. "But I didn't get much done as my gout started acting up and I had to drive to Beamsville to see the doctor." She blushed as she said it.

Ruth assured her it was okay, got the letter, and hurried out of the store. She used the main street to get to Saul's for a change, holding the envelope very prominently in her hand so anyone watching would know why she was going there. She went to the front porch, too, and rapped on the screen door. The inside door opened and Saul gave her a what-are-you-doing-here look.

"Sam asked me to drop this letter off. You missed it when you got the mail this morning," she said loud enough for anyone to hear.

Saul's face darkened. "Thanks," he muttered, taking it without looking at it. He shoved it in his jeans pocket. Ruth eyed him suspiciously.

"You didn't miss this in the box, did you? You purposely left it in there." Ruth could not be fooled when it came to people pretending. She could see it in their eyes or the way they moved. Like the time her dad gave her mom a scale for her birthday, because he knew she was watching her weight. Her mom pretended to be pleased, but Ruth was very aware of her mother's strained smile and the way she wouldn't look at her dad. Ruth wasn't at all surprised to see the never-used scale in a cardboard box in the garage destined for donations. She was also not surprised to see her father's least favorite meal of cabbage rolls on the supper table at least once a week after that.

Saul was clearly upset. His shoulders were hunched and his left hand clenched in and out of a fist.

"Who's it from?" she asked.

Saul took a long time to answer. "Some distant relatives of Aunt Bea's. They've hired a lawyer. They say Aunt Bea wasn't in her right mind when she left the house to us."

Ruth sucked in her breath. "But why? Is it their life's dream to live in a house with old plumbing and bad Internet?"

"Dad won't say much, but they seem to think Aunt Bea was loaded or something and that a lot of money was hidden in the house. They keep sending threatening letters, demanding we leave."

"What does your dad say?"

Saul shrugged. "Dad keeps saying we haven't done anything wrong, but he gets really upset every time one of those letters arrives. I just wanted to spare him another round of stress."

"Sorry. Didn't mean to make things worse," she said. "I'm sure it will all work out." Ruth pasted a smile on her face, but she wasn't sure at all. And suddenly the idea that Saul might have to leave made her stomach lurch.

It was time to change the subject with Saul.

"What do you think of this?" she asked, taking a quick look around to see who might be watching from the street before pulling the brooch out of her pocket. She held it low just in case Mrs. Gorgonzola was in her front room rocker, watching them.

"What is it? It's so covered in clay I can't tell."

"It's a brooch. If you hold it up to the light, you can see there's a dark red stone in the middle."

"Where'd you get it?"

"By the Old Parish Church ruins."

Saul turned it over in his hand. "Wait here," he said and went inside, leaving Ruth to stand uncomfortably on the porch as neighbors walked, biked, or drove by. She felt like a thousand eyes were on her.

Saul came back holding a very different-looking brooch. "I washed it off as best I could."

Ruth took the brooch and her jaw dropped. This was no dollar store pin dropped by a hiker. This looked old, really old. Ruth ran her finger over the detailed gold edging surrounding a large red stone.

"Do you think it's a real gem? It's awfully big," Ruth said.

Saul shrugged. "What would I know about jewelry? But if it *is* real, then maybe what we're really looking for …"

Ruth could almost feel Mrs. Gorgonzola whispering in her ear as she finished the thought for him, "… is treasure."

⁓ Chapter 17 ⁓

Ruth rolled the idea around in her head as she perched in the maple tree. Treasure. Was that what Bea was hiding? Maybe Bea's relatives were right. Maybe the tunnel led to a buried horde of gold and jewels. Ruth would have suspected Bea's relatives except Mrs. Gorgonzola was adamant that no strangers were in Pinkerton the day Bea disappeared. Knowing of a buried treasure certainly would put a target on someone's back. That gave Ruth the shivers, and she almost slipped off her branch. If someone suspected she knew where it was, Bea would be right and she could be next.

Despite the dangers, Ruth allowed herself to imagine what a treasure worth thousands or maybe millions of dollars would do to her life. Maybe her family could buy a big farm. Her mom could have the garden of her dreams and Ruth could have a huge flock of chickens. Maybe even a horse. Or Alpacas. Her heart quickened. She could buy her brothers the sickest game system with so many games that they would be so wrapped up in them they would never bug her again. Her dad would want to travel. Maybe they could all go to the Pyramids in Egypt? The possibilities were endless.

"So why didn't Bea?" Saul asked at the chicken coop that night, when Ruth excitedly told him all the things she would do with her riches. He leaned against the wall and then jumped off, frantically brushing at the sleeve of his sweater with his hand.

"It's not a worm," Ruth said automatically, although it was too dark to see for sure. "Why didn't Bea what?"

"Move. Travel. Get better clothes. Eat caviar. Gold-plate her toilet. Anything."

It was a good question. Why didn't Bea act like someone who was rich if she had access to buried treasure? Even if she didn't want to flash ruby brooches around, she could pawn small pieces here and there to make her life easier. But Bea lived a completely ordinary life, growing her own vegetables, using coupons at the store, mending holes in her sweaters. It didn't add up.

"Maybe there's no treasure after all," Ruth said, her shoulders drooping in disappointment. "Maybe this is all just a coincidence — Bea drowning, the tunnel, the key."

"Or maybe it has something to do with the church's architect, Thomas Fuller."

"You mean the name that was underlined in her book? What could be interesting about an architect?"

"The fact that he was a Freemason."

Ruth looked up in surprise. "Aren't Freemasons a super-secret group? They blow up buildings or something, don't they? Or are they the ones that wear robes and hide in caves?" Was this the cult Mrs. Gorgonzola suspected? Were all her theories correct? Being right about all her conspiracies would make Mrs. Gorgonzola more insufferable than ever.

"Neither," Saul said. "They just have private meetings that they don't talk about."

"I think there's more to it than that," Ruth said. "The men who belong to it are probably felons or something, hiding from the law."

"No, they're not. They're ordinary men."

"What makes you so sure?"

Saul shuffled his feet a little. "My dad's a Freemason. Those are the meetings he goes to in Beamsville."

Ruth said nothing. She winced inside. She had basically just called Saul's dad a criminal. Ruth figured this was why she didn't have many friends. She also realized she was on the hook for another apology.

"Why is it important that the architect was a Free-mason?" Ruth asked, and then, not wanting her insult to hang between them, added without practicing first, "and sorry, I didn't mean to imply your dad did anything wrong."

Saul shrugged. "That's okay. I'm not sure how or why Freemasons are involved, but Fuller's name must have been underlined for some reason."

"So where are we with this?" Ruth said. "Bea had a caved-in tunnel under her house that led to the ruins of a church built by a Freemason. We have a brooch that could be gold found near the entrance to the tunnel and a key that doesn't open anything we can find."

"Don't forget we have a solid suspect in Sam," Saul said.

"Right, but if he *did it* …" Ruth could never bring herself to actually say the words *murdered her*, "… was it because of the goats or because of the treasure?"

"We're not even sure there *is* a treasure," Saul reminded her. "But we *know* Sam sold his goats because of Bea."

"But why would Bea be worried about me being the next victim if this was about the goats? Sam wouldn't target me; I had nothing to do with it," Ruth said. "A treasure makes more sense if someone thought Bea passed on to me where it was."

"I guess," Saul admitted.

"Do Freemasons have a lot of loot? Did Thomas Fuller hide something in his church?"

Saul shook his head. "I told you … just ordinary men. But some say they were connected to another secret group — the Templars. And they *did* have incredible treasure."

Ruth held up a hand and froze. "Someone is coming," she said in the barest whisper. They moved closer to the coop, pressing their backs against the wall. Ruth prayed the hens wouldn't sense their presence and start clucking and drawing attention to them. They heard a couple of twigs snap to their left, close to the woods.

"Is it one of your brothers?" Saul whispered.

"I don't think so. They can't walk two feet without yelling," Ruth replied. They stood silently, straining to hear.

"Look," Ruth whispered. "Over there."

In the deepening gloom they could see movement. A black shadow glided from the edge of the woods, past her mother's lilac bushes and headed toward the house.

"I wish that motion-sensing porch light was still working," Ruth muttered.

"Should we make some noise and scare them off?" Saul asked.

"No." Ruth wanted to know who was creeping around their house. The figure was bent over, so it was impossible to guess their height, but it definitely wasn't a kid. The shadow neared a bit of light from the den window that came through the curtains and brightened a small patch of ground. Ruth hoped that the light would give the sneak away. A couple more steps and Ruth would have her answer. Whoever it was, they took one step closer and the light bounced off something in their hand.

Ruth gasped. It was a crowbar.

"Bwrack!"

Behind them, Dorcas stood in the still-open door of the coop and raised the alarm. The hens, who were normally roosting quietly were now all clucking and flapping. Ruth cursed whichever brother it was who forgot to close up the coop. Brothers were so unreliable.

The shadow stopped, spun and took off back towards the woods.

"Should we chase them?" Saul asked, moving away from the wall, ready to run.

"Are you crazy? Didn't you see the weapon in their hand? One bash of a crowbar on the skull and it's lights out, for good."

The sounds of twigs snapping and the vibrations of footfalls faded as the intruder ran off. The hens finally quieted down and marched back up the ramp into their coop. Ruth lowered the door.

She and Saul stood in the darkness, coming to grips with what had just happened. Was it a thief, looking to break into Ruth's house? That was pretty hard to believe. The last break-in in Pinkerton was five years ago when Mr. and Mrs. Gorgonzola came back from Bingo Night at the church hall to find their front door standing open. Inside the house, all the cupboards and drawers were open and everything was thrown on the floors. The police from Beamsville were called, but after a long cleanup, the only thing missing was Mrs. Gorgonzola's ugly neon green lava lamp. A few weeks later Sam saw it for sale on eBay. Mrs. Gorgonzola was able to buy it back for one dollar because there were no other bids. Whispers around Pinkerton were that Mr. Gorgonzola had staged the whole break-in to get rid of the lamp, which mysteriously broke only a few days after Mrs. Gorgonzola bought it back.

So if not a burglar, was it something more sinister? Despite Saul and Ruth's care not to make their connection obvious and put a target on Ruth's back, maybe someone was suspicious. All Ruth could see in her mind was the glint of the light on that heavy, metal crowbar. Wondering if it had been meant for her, Ruth shivered uncontrollably.

The thought struck her that Dorcas may have just saved her life.

⮬ Chapter 18 ⮪

It was the day Ruth had been dreading all summer: the Sharpe family reunion and picnic. It would be nice, she reasoned, to have a day off from trying to figure out cryptic clues and solve a murder all while looking over her shoulder for attackers with crowbars. Still, a trip to the beach would have done a better job of that than this jock-fest laced with creamy coleslaw and bug spray.

Her brothers couldn't wait to join their cousins in the quest for the Sharpe-of-the-Year trophy, which was nothing more than a plastic Rock'em Sock'em robot nailed to a block of wood. But you would think it was a gold-plated Oscar the way they fought over every point from dumb picnic games to take that piece of junk home for the year. Abe had won it two years ago, and paraded it around the house pressing the button to make the robot punch and saying "KaPOW" for months. For her birthday, Ruth asked that her present be that the trophy be banned from the downstairs. The following year it was George who won it. Ruth didn't want to give up another birthday present so she hid the thing in the chicken coop until George found it during a game of hide and seek. Ruth was terrified that one of her brothers would win it again. She wondered how ethical it would be to spike their lemonade with sleep-inducing cold medication to help them lose so she could have a year of peace.

As the enormous Sharpe family took over Riverside Park, Ruth settled down under a tree with a book to endure the day. This was the time to put her invisibility to good use. If she stayed still and silent, engrossed in *A Wrinkle in Time* and how Meg and Charles Wallace were going to rescue their father from the planet Camazotz, maybe no one would see her and try to talk to her. Her mother's family was large, loud, and boisterous, and Ruth could only tolerate them one or two at a time. The whole bunch of them was a thing to be avoided at any cost.

Except for hunger.

Ruth's one weakness was picnic food. When the food came out, so did Ruth. She had to elbow her way to the table to snag some of her mom's potato salad before it was all gone. Her cousin Dana was hogging the spoon so she had to wait for an opportune moment to snatch it out of her hand before Dana passed it to someone else. Getting food was a contest of wits. In fact, everything was a competition for the Sharpes.

"So, Marie," Ruth heard her Aunt Lily say to her mother as she scooped coleslaw, "how does this compare to the Mornay picnic?"

"Uh, they don't have one."

Ruth heard a metal spoon clatter onto a plate as her aunt dropped it in surprise. "What do you mean, they don't have one? I thought you said Anton had a large family?"

"He does, five brothers."

Ruth moved out of their line of sight, but where she could still hear them.

Aunt Lily lowered her voice. "You'd think Ruth would be enough reason to get together. I mean, the first girl born in two generations?"

Her mother shrugged. "The only one to make a fuss was his grandmother, Hildie. She was thrilled. Anton was her favorite after that. I think when she left her property to us and not the others, they took offence. Said they were going to contest the will. They wanted the money. They never did though. Not once they found out that there was a provision in Hildie's will that the property could not be sold outside the family. None of them wanted to live in Pinkerton."

Aunt Lily sniffed. "Never understood people who hold a grudge. Like Mable. Did you see that she brought a pineapple upside down cake even though she knew I was bringing one? Just because she brings one every year doesn't mean we shouldn't change it up now and then. And besides, do you see that there's one more piece gone out of mine than hers?"

Ruth took her paper plate, which was groaning with food, back to the tree. She tried to digest, not only her lunch, but what she had just heard. When she was working on her family history project and asked her Dad about any relatives beyond his parents, Gerard and Anna Mornay, he told her he really didn't know anything. In the end, on the day Bea disappeared, she turned it in even though the tree was pretty bare (and got a C+). Now it turns out he was close to his grandmother Hildie, and she left him the property they now live on in Pinkerton. Why did he pretend he didn't know her? And if her great-grandmother Hildie was excited Ruth was the first girl in two generations, why didn't Ruth remember going to visit her? Unless she died when Ruth was just a baby. But her name was never even mentioned.

None of it made sense. It was time for some more sleuthing when she got home. She needed the Internet. It was no use asking her dad to use his computer for this because if he was unwilling to tell her anything when she asked him to his face, he probably would come up with an excuse to not let her use it. And the nearest public library with computers was in

Beamsville. But there was someone with their own computer and unlimited Internet — Saul. It would mean sneaking over to his house, but Ruth felt a burning curiosity about Great-grandmother Hildie and the rest of the Mornays. Something wasn't right.

"I need a partner."

Ruth looked up at the nasally voice. It was her cousin Dana.

"Get lost. I'm reading," Ruth said.

"FYI: They get their father back and Charles Wallace starts talking."

Ruth slammed the book closed. "That was nasty. But seeing as I've read the book before, it's not a spoiler. The question is, how do you know the ending? I bet you've never read a complete book in your life."

Dana, who apparently had skin so thick she didn't care when she was being insulted, shrugged. "I saw the movie," she said. "Are you coming? I need a partner for the three-legged race."

Ruth tilted her head. "How are my brothers doing?"

"George has the most points out of all of them, but he hasn't won anything yet. If he wins this race, he's pretty much got the trophy in the bag."

Ruth got up and brushed off her shorts. "Let's go. And you better be fast."

Terror at the thought of another year of "KaPOW" had Ruth flying down the course and propelling them to a victory. After this loss, George never recovered the point lead and Dana walked off with the trophy. The day had a bonus result of George not speaking to Ruth for weeks.

Ruth wondered if wanting distance from your family was something she inherited from her dad. Maybe that's why he never told her about Great-grandmother Hildie. Maybe he was embarrassed about his family because of the bad feelings over the will. Or maybe he was just getting forgetful.

Ruth hoped that it was forgetfulness and not what her gut was telling her — that it was something far deeper and far darker.

ᗌ Chapter 19 ᗎ

It had been tricky finding a time to sneak over to Saul's house to use his computer, but luckily his dad had another Freemason meeting that Wednesday night. They both stared at the screen.

"What am I looking at?" Ruth asked. Saul had logged on to a family tree site that had records and documents. He searched the words *Mornay* and *Pinkerton*.

"It's a list of the people living in Pinkerton in 1911. A census."

A name jumped out at Ruth.

"Mornay. Look. Right there: Francis Mornay. What does the 'HH' mean?" she asked.

"*Head of Household*, it says at the top."

"And below his name is Hildegard Mornay. That must be Hildie. And one, two, three ... seven sons." Ruth read the names looking for her grandfather's name. "There he is ...

Gerard, 8 months old. But who is this at the end of the list living with them? It says MIL."

"Mother-in-law."

"Hildie's mother lived with them? Wait a minute … her name was Clara *Payens*?"

Ruth and Saul stared in disbelief. "It can't be a coincidence, right? Hildie's maiden name being the same as Bea's last name? They had to be related, right?" Ruth asked.

Ruth tried to untangle all the information in her head, but it was a knot of confusion. All these people were her relatives, but she had never heard of them even though their names were just a couple of computer clicks away. One thing became crystal clear: her father was holding back on her.

The real question was, she thought to herself, should she confront her dad? Would he confess that he knew more than he was saying?

"I think he'll stick to his story about not knowing much if you ask him," Saul said when she asked him what he thought she should do. "You can find more online than he'll ever admit to, anyway. And besides, the more interesting question is *why* he is trying to keep this information from you and if you let him know you're on to him, you might never find out."

Ruth and Saul explored the website looking for more

information on the Mornays of Pinkerton, but all of a sudden, the trail went cold. They couldn't find out where the family lived before they moved to the village.

Ruth went home, a headache brewing. She wondered if her acting skills were up to behaving like everything was normal around her dad. Acting as if it didn't feel like her whole world was spinning out of control. Ruth wished she were smarter. Then she would have already figured out what Bea was trying to tell her and what she felt she needed to warn her about. Right now, there were more questions than answers.

Ruth was spared any awkwardness with her dad because he wasn't home when she got back. She took two steps up the staircase to go to her room and paused. Her dad's office was in the small space that was originally the pantry next to the kitchen. If there were anything that might answer some questions about the Mornays, it would be in there.

She lost her nerve. If her mom or any of her brothers caught her in there, they would tell her dad and who knows how mad he'd be ... especially if whatever this was, was supposed to be a secret. But still, her foot wouldn't climb even one more step. She had to know. She turned and snuck into the cramped room.

Her dad's desk was so littered with papers and files that she almost couldn't see the desk at all. She carefully lifted the papers trying not to move them too much. There was nothing in sight except bank account papers and letters from an insurance company. Ruth stopped moving to hear if anyone was coming. All was quiet. She went to an oak filing cabinet jammed between the desk and the wall. It only had old bills and insurance forms. She tried the three desk drawers. They had office supplies, computer cables, and old bills.

Ruth heard footsteps approaching. She went silent, holding her breath. They stopped. Ruth heard a sigh that was without a doubt her mother's. Her mother sighed a lot. It was usually over cereal bowls not being rinsed, shoes blocking the door, and board game miniatures left on the floor that crippled anyone who walked on them.

The footsteps moved on. Ruth breathed again. She looked around the room. There wasn't really anywhere else to look, except for the bookcase. There were some history books and a few tax manuals. The rest were science fiction novels. *This is a waste of time,* Ruth thought. She wasn't sure what she thought she might find in there. It's not like her dad had a complete family tree hanging on the wall for her to find.

Then she saw something out of place — a leather-bound book of Shakespeare's sonnets in between Adams' *The Hitchhiker's Guide to the Galaxy* and Asimov's *Foundation*. Her father might be a man of secrets, but one thing everyone knew — her dad hated Shakespeare and his "gobbledygook

English," as he called it. In a tiny room with limited book-shelf space, there's no way he would take up so much as an inch for a book by Shakespeare.

She pulled it off the shelf. It was too light for a real book. Sure enough, the inside of the book had been cut out, leaving only page edges around a hiding space. In it sat a small, brown envelope. Ruth took it out and carefully opened the brittle flap and pulled out a piece of lined paper. There was handwriting on it that she didn't recognize. She started reading:

I, Hildegard Mornay, being of sound mind but frail of body ...

It was Great-grandmother Hildie's will. The one the family fought over. Ruth read on to where Hildie granted her sons certain items like furniture, jewelry, pictures, chests, and dishes. Small things. And then came the line where her grandson and Ruth's father, Anton, got all of the family property and house. But as Ruth read the last line on the page, her heart started to pound:

And to my great-granddaughter, Ruth, as she is destined to carry the burden ...

Ruth turned over the page, but it was blank. She opened the envelope again, figuring the second page was stuck inside, but inside was empty. The rest of the will was missing.

Ruth heard thumps and bumps as one or two of her

brothers bounded into the kitchen, near the office door. She replaced the page in the envelope and put it back in its hiding spot inside the book on the shelf. When the noises moved off, she slipped out of the office and headed upstairs.

She trembled as she got ready for bed. The words *destined to carry the burden* were burned into her mind. Up until now, her curiosity was driving her to find answers. Now she wondered if maybe it would be better not to know the truth after all.

❧ Chapter 20 ❧

Feeling that somehow her family history mystery and Bea's death were connected, Ruth turned her attention back to figuring out who had a motive to harm Bea. Saul and Ruth agreed that she should be the one to try and feel Sam out — see what he had to say about where he was the day Bea disappeared and how much anger he might be harboring about his goats. It was going to be tricky, though … Ruth hadn't yet forgotten the sight of him with a long knife in his hand. She got her chance when she was sent to the store a couple of days later. This time Ruth's mother needed mushroom soup and garbage bags.

Harriet Ings was at her usual post behind the counter. "Oh, I was so hoping I'd see you!" Harriet said, clasping her hands together. "I have the hat I made for you." She reached behind the counter and pulled it out.

Ruth took the wide-brimmed straw hat and her breath caught in her throat. It was an exact replica of Bea's. Ruth had seen her wear it a thousand times when she was out in her garden. A red band circled the crown and it was covered with flowers, including roses of course, they were Bea's favorite.

"Bea asked for these exact flowers?" Ruth asked.

"Yup. She insisted on pink roses, white lilies, forget-me-nots, and Solomon's seal flowers all on a red band. You have no idea how difficult it was to find artificial Solomon's seal flowers. I wanted to substitute something similar, but she said no." Harriet sighed. "I found some online and had to have them shipped. But Beatrice said she would pay whatever it cost."

"Why was it so important?"

"I don't know. But she was so picky. The forget-me-nots had to be the right shade of blue, the roses had to be pink, and the lilies, white. They weren't easy to find, I tell you."

Ruth carefully placed the hat on her head.

"Oh," Harriet said, putting a hand to her mouth. "For a second there, you looked a bit like Beatrice. How extraordinary."

That made Ruth happy and sad at the same time. And more determined than ever to find out what happened to her friend.

"Is Sam here?" Ruth asked.

Harriet Ings shook her head. "He's away at a show. Do you

need to order something? I can help with that."

"No," Ruth said, frustrated that she was going to have to wait to question Sam when she had finally worked up the nerve to talk to him. "When will he be back?"

"Well, the show runs all weekend, so Monday."

"What show?"

"Rabbit show. He's going for the high point trophy. They've done really well this year."

"Sam has rabbits? When did this happen?"

"Right after he sold the goats. Says it's the best thing that ever happened to him and he wishes he had done it a long time ago. His Angora rabbits are winning awards left, right, and center. Sam says it makes their fur even more valuable."

Ruth didn't know what to say. Sam was keeping and showing Angora rabbits? And wished he'd done it sooner? Didn't sound too much like a man harboring a grudge against Bea for the loss of his goats.

Mr. Weeks came up behind Ruth with a bag of oranges and a loaf of bread. "That's quite a hat," he said with a smile. "Haven't I seen it before?"

"It's just like Beatrice's," Harriet Ings said proudly. "I made them both."

"Ah, that's it." He turned to Ruth. "Odd choice of hat for a girl. Don't you kids all wear ball caps or something?"

"It's … it's a present for my mother," Ruth lied, smiling

at both of them. She didn't need Harriet Ings spreading it around Pinkerton that it was Ruth who wanted a copy of Bea's hat. Someone might get suspicious. And luckily, Harriet Ings was too busy ringing in Mr. Weeks's items to ask any more nosy questions.

She plucked the hat back off, grabbed the bag of groceries, and headed home. She hoped Saul would show up at the coop at dusk, although she didn't have any good news for him. Another suspect seemed to have gone down the drain. If Sam wasn't bitter that he had to sell his goats because he was doing so well with his rabbits, then he really had no motive. Although frustrated that she couldn't figure this out, Ruth was a little relieved that it wasn't Sam. She hoped that it was still somehow an escaped prisoner on the run through town or a tourist gone crazy. Anyone but the people she had grown up with.

Ruth made sure the coop door was down and the hens were in for the night as she waited for Saul. She didn't want a repeat of the other night with the intruder. The memory kept her on high alert as she tried to listen for footsteps coming through the woods over the sound of the light rain that was falling. This time though, she was prepared. Her hand closed on the cold metal handle of her own weapon.

"Are you planning on flipping burgers?" Saul asked, coming around the corner of the coop.

Ruth put the large metal spatula behind her back. "It's all I could grab out of the drainboard while my mom's back was turned. I … I wanted some protection."

"It's too bad you didn't have Bratwurst for supper. Then you could at least have a meat fork to stab your attacker."

"Don't joke about this," Ruth snapped. "Someone was creeping around our house in the dark with a lethal weapon a few days ago."

Saul looked at the ground. "I'm sorry. I wasn't making fun of you. I, uh, had the same thought." He pulled a wrench out of his back pocket. "If nothing else we can swat mosquitos and put furniture together."

Ruth laughed and then covered her mouth. Ruth told Saul what she had found out about Sam.

"That's a dead end then," he said. "We have no idea who Aunt Bea's killer is."

Ruth listened to the crickets sing while she thought about that. "But *she* did," she said.

"Pardon?"

"You said Bea knew she was going to be murdered. She must have had some idea of who it was." She looked at Saul. "She knew where the danger was and left us clues. We need to work out what she was trying to tell us."

"Well, the Old Parish Church must be important because she left us the glove map to it."

"And the key that was hidden in the frog must mean something too." Ruth pulled the chain out from under her sweater. She ran her fingers over the key, imagining Bea doing the same. That's when she felt it.

"Give me your phone," Ruth said. Saul dug in his pocket and handed it to her. She turned on the flashlight and trained the light onto the shaft of the key.

"What are you looking for?" Saul asked.

"I felt something. Like faint lines. But I can't see anything."

"Let me try." Saul took the key and the phone and stared at it. "It's pretty faint."

Ruth bent down and scooped up a tiny bit of reddish-brown clay mud. She rubbed it over the lines on the shaft and then used the sleeve of her sweater to gently remove the excess. "Is that better?" The mud made the lines stand out against the brass.

CT VI 3922

Ruth and Saul looked at each other and shook their heads.

"It doesn't mean anything to me," Saul said.

"But it must have meant something to Bea. She hid it in the frog for a reason." Ruth had a strange feeling that this was, literally and figuratively, the key to everything.

Chapter 21

The rain kept up all the next day. And the next. Ruth did manage to escape the house to the maple tree for about an hour while the rain just drizzled and the leaves kept her mostly dry. She'd had another one of her vivid nightmares the night before and although she couldn't really remember it, she was still overwhelmed with the feeling of impending doom. Ruth tried to recall any details, but every time she thought she had latched onto something, it unraveled again and drifted away.

A drop of rain made it past the leafy canopy and dripped on her forehead. As it hit her skin, she could feel ice cold water soaking her shoes and then rising up to her ankles. She looked down, expecting to see herself standing in water, but of course that was impossible — she was up a tree. The feeling disappeared, but it brought back her dream from the night before. Water. That was it. It had to do with water.

But was the rising water a memory of Bea's death, or a warning about her own?

From her perch, Ruth watched the comings and goings in Pinkerton. Mr. Parker got gas at Sam's. Harriet Ings walked home for lunch under her big yellow umbrella. Mr. Weeks rode by on his bike, his raincoat flapping out behind him. Mrs. Parsons picked up a few things at the store and ran to her car, her handbag over her head. And then Ruth noticed Mrs. Gorgonzola rocking in her chair inside her front window: watching everything and everyone.

"Mrs. Gorgonzola might have a clue as to what happened to Bea," Ruth said to Saul that night at the coop. "She's always sitting in her front window, watching. And she's nosy. When she's outside, she talks to anyone who walks slowly enough for her to catch up to."

"I already spoke to her once."

"I know, but she was Bea's neighbor for twenty years. And I hate to admit it, but a lot of the things she whispered about Bea seem to have some nugget of truth. I would bet anything she knows more than she's said so far. And people always remember more details when they're questioned a second time. You'd know that if you'd watch more mystery shows."

"Soooo you're going to go talk to her this time?"

"No way. I checked out Sam and Mrs. Ings."

Saul's shoulders drooped. "She scares me."

"Suck it up, Buttercup," Ruth said. "Bea involved you in this when she wrote to you and asked you to contact me."

"What am I supposed to ask Mrs. Gorgonzola?"

"Ask her about the last time she saw Bea. Did Bea say anything about being afraid? Did she see anything unusual that day? That sort of thing. Seriously, I can give you a list of shows to watch."

"No thanks. I'll wing it."

Ruth harumphed, hoping Saul was up to the job.

"Any luck deciphering the code on the key?" she asked.

"I did a search of people with those initials. Lots of movie stars, but none of the names really jumped out at me."

"A phrase then?"

"Like what? Crawl tunnel? Climb tower?"

"Maybe," Ruth said, but she knew in her gut that that wasn't it.

"I'll keep looking," Saul said. "Meanwhile, watch your back."

"What do you mean?"

"Someone's been in our house again."

"What was it this time? Your T-shirts were crumpled? Cereal boxes moved?"

"No. Bea's books on the bookshelves were out of order."

"There's an order to her books?"

"Yup, first by subject and then alphabetical. Four of them

were put back wrong. Someone's been going through them," Saul said.

Ruth didn't bother to ask him if he were sure, otherwise she'd get another lecture on his eidetic memory. She couldn't imagine what it would be like to be able to look at something and then have an image of that burned in your memory forever. Forget studying for a test … everything would be right there and you'd just have to scroll through it like your picture file on your computer. Ruth figured Saul must be the smartest kid in school.

"Have you checked the books? Is there anything inside them?" Ruth couldn't help but think about the cutout book on her dad's shelves.

"I did. There's nothing unusual. No cavities. No photos or letters in between the pages. No handwritten notes. Nothing."

Ruth felt a shiver of anxiety. Then it changed to anger. How dare someone just break into someone else's house and wander around. The rule in Pinkerton was that an unlocked door was *not* an invitation to come in. Ruth had had enough. "I think it's time to set a trap."

Ruth's plan was a daring one. Saul's cello lesson was that Friday and this time, they were going to be ready. Ruth took her time sneaking over to Saul's house Friday afternoon, taking a long route through the woods and the fields to get to his house. Saul's father worked from home, but luckily, he had errands to run in Beamsville, so Ruth and Saul could get to work.

"Don't forget the side windows," Ruth told Saul as he put a small piece of clear tape over the openings of each door and window. The only one that wouldn't have one would be the front door where Saul would exit after his dad was already in the car. But Ruth figured someone sneaking around wouldn't use that door, anyway.

"Did you remember the baby powder?" Saul asked.

"Yup. But you'll have to sprinkle it quickly right before you leave and your dad is out of the house."

"Everywhere?" he asked.

"No, just on the white tile floor in the kitchen. If anyone walks on it, they'll track it all through the house." Ruth carefully laid a strand of black thread on the top of cupboard doors and drawers. Then she wiped down the doorknobs on every door on the main floor. "If anyone touches them, we can dust for prints."

"Do you know how to do that?"

"I looked it up at the library once, when my brothers kept taking stuff from my room. My dad said he couldn't punish them unless he knew which one it was. So I found out for him."

They finished up and Ruth snuck back home. Was someone really breaking in or was Saul just paranoid? And if someone *had* been snooping around, would they come back? What were they looking for?

Ruth could barely sleep that night, wondering what Saul had found when he came back from his cello lessons. He had told her he would make sure he was first inside and take photos on his phone of anything he found. She finally drifted off to sleep, convinced that even if Saul wasn't letting his imagination get out of control, it was highly unlikely anything would happen that night.

She was wrong.

⌁ Chapter 22 ⌁

"What do you mean, you're not sure if anyone was there?" Ruth asked, folding her arms and leaning against the rough boards of the coop. Inside, the hens cooed as they fluttered onto their roosts for the night. "Isn't that why we did all that?"

Saul sighed. "When we got home, my dad had to go, bad. He took off for the bathroom in through the kitchen door before I could get in front of him. He raced across the tile floor, kicking up powder, without even taking his shoes off. If there had been any footprints, they were gone."

"What about the tape on the windows and doors?"

"Well, I don't know about the back door because of dad bursting through it, but none of the others seemed to be touched. But …" Saul paused, scrunching up his face like he wasn't sure whether or not he should go on.

"But what?"

"Well, there was something odd. The basement door was closed with the tape still on it, but I had to go down there for more toilet paper and there was a bit of powder on the first couple of steps."

"Did your dad go into the basement?"

"No."

"Could the powder have blown in under the door?"

"Nope. There's a rubber sweep on the bottom. Probably put there to keep out drafts."

"So how could there be powder if no one went down there?"

Saul shrugged. "It doesn't make any sense."

"Unless …" Ruth's forehead wrinkled, "… someone *did* break in, saw the powder, and tried to avoid it while going to the basement. They also saw the tape, so when they left, they stuck it back on the doorframe again."

"If that's the case, then this is no ordinary intruder. This is someone who knows what they're doing. There's one other thing: if they stuck the tape back on the door …"

"They would have left a fingerprint!" Ruth said. "Do you still have the tape?"

Saul nodded. "It's still there. I didn't have time to take it all off with dad working in the kitchen."

"Use tweezers to take it off. Put it in a jar or something."

"But I touched it when I put it up there. My fingerprints will be on it, too."

"Probably just on the edges and we can rule those out. There's still a chance we'll have a solid print."

"Yeah but how do we identify who it is? How did you do it with your brothers?"

"I took juice glasses that each of them touched and compared them."

"Great. Once we have the print, we just need to collect the fingerprints of every resident in Pinkerton without them knowing we're doing it. Easy."

"You know, sarcasm doesn't suit you," Ruth said, her hands on her hips. "We could start with likely suspects. George has a microscope we can use to compare any that we find."

Saul sighed. "All right. I'll get it tonight. But if we're dealing with someone this sneaky, Bea was right, and we, or I guess you, are in real danger."

Ruth tried to act like it didn't frighten her, but inside her stomach was churning. All along she had let herself hold a kernel of hope inside that Bea's death was an accident. But more and more it was looking like someone sinister was lurking in quiet Pinkerton.

Saul left to go home and collect the tape from the basement door and Ruth went back inside. But not until after first standing inside the dark doorway and peering back out into the yard looking for movement. She still hadn't gotten over the mysterious shadow person from the other night with the crowbar. Back up in her room, she slipped off the chain holding the key over her head and studied it. Bea had been trying to tell her something. If only she could figure out what. She pulled the embroidered gloves out from her night table and laid them on her bed. She put down the key and with her finger, traced the embroidered lines on the gloves, seeing a map of Pinkerton in her mind portrayed in the design. It was amazing how exactly the thread vine mimicked the road through the village. She noticed that the location of each building in Pinkerton seemed to be represented by a different flower. Bea's was the rose, of course. It was no surprise to Ruth that Bea had asked for them to be on her hat too. Where St. Ignatius would be, was a small, star-shaped flower with five petals. Her house, the Mornay property, had a clump of tiny flowers. They looked a little like the blooms on her mother's lilac bushes. Near the X or cross of the Old Parish Church, there was a little group of three long bell-like flowers. Ruth stared at them. They looked a lot like the Solomon's seal flowers on Bea's hat.

Ruth ran to get the straw hat from her closet and set it on the bed next to the gloves and the key. The flowers were an exact match. Ruth moved the gloves next to each other to allow the embroidered vine road to continue from one glove to the other. That's when she noticed the blank space that spanned them. It was a familiar shape. Ruth picked up the key and set it down perfectly in the blank space across the gloves.

She was excited. Another clue! But what did it mean? What was the connection between the key and this spot on the map? She shook her head. She couldn't figure it out.

But one other little idea niggled at the back of her mind. The flowers. The flowers seemed to be important: each different one on the gloves and the detailed instructions for the hat. For not the first time, Ruth wished her parents were a little more flexible with letting her and her brothers have Internet access in the house, but they were convinced it was unnecessary and full of nonsense that would "rot their brains." It was always so uncomfortable to have to ask permission to use her dad's computer. He was so paranoid that they would download a virus that would wipe out all his files. He constantly checked his browser history. It would be nearly impossible to do a search on the hidden meanings of flowers, let alone the Freemasons or her own family tree without her dad finding out. She knew getting to the public library in Beamsville was next to impossible. She would have to sneak over to Saul's again.

Footsteps came up the stairs and down the hallway. Her parents were going to bed.

"Lights out, Ruth," her mother said through the closed door.

"Okay," Ruth answered.

She put the key and the gloves in her night table drawer and lay back on her bed to think. Those items seemed so ordinary and meaningless when she first got them, but now Ruth realized they were more than they seemed.

She sat bolt upright in bed. The ugly hair picture. Maybe there was more to that too. She waited until she was sure her parents were in bed and asleep and crept downstairs to the den. She switched on one of the lamps and closed the door so the light wouldn't be obvious to anyone making a bathroom run upstairs. She took the picture down from the wall and sat on the horsehair sofa to study it.

It was still ugly. Knowing each petal was someone's hair made her gag just a little. She took a deep breath and focused on the picture. It looked like a bouquet of flowers in a vase and this time she noticed that the flowers were all five-petaled like the ones on the gloves and the white lilies on the straw hat. Ruth also noticed that one large flower in the middle of the hair picture was surrounded by identically sized flowers all around in a perfect circle. The one at the top of the picture was the unfinished one, with with petals missing on the flower. Something about the image gave her shivers. There was something about the pattern of petals and stems. She turned the frame over and saw that the backing was held in place by little metal tabs. She bent them outward and pulled the backing off. She held the back of the picture up for a better look, seeing a pattern made by the threads holding the hair on the front in place. The arcs and circles reminded her of intricate designs in the adult coloring books in the rack at the Gas 'n' Go, called mandalas. She looked closely at it. The mandala seemed to pulse and grow brighter. Her vision narrowed, and she felt sweaty and lightheaded. She could feel the blood draining from her face.

That's when Ruth blacked out.

∽ Chapter 23 ∾

Ruth wasn't sure how long she had lain there, slumped over on the horsehair sofa. She could see that the picture had slipped from her hands and landed face up on the floor. She got up, holding the armrest of the sofa in case she was still woozy, but she felt fine.

What had happened? She strained to remember. She had flipped the picture over and then …

"Hallucination," she told herself. A design doesn't pulse. She picked the picture up. "No, I think this is important."

She turned the image over again. Then she carefully and deliberately looked at the mandala made by the threads. The pattern didn't move this time, but looking at it felt almost as if Bea were reaching out and touching her arm. She shivered.

She replaced the picture in its frame, hung it back on the wall, turned out the light and climbed the stairs to her room. In bed, she fell into a deep but restless sleep. She had another of her nightmares.

Ruth couldn't remember what she had dreamt, but she woke up exhausted and anxious. The rain pelting against her bedroom window didn't help her mood. She skipped breakfast and grabbed her raincoat and went outside figuring rain or no rain, she would feel better in her maple tree breathing some fresh air.

She sat in her perch for quite a while, letting the breeze blow over her. Movement across the road by the priest's house caught her eye. Standing near the door to the rectory, which adjoined St. Ignatius at the rear of the church, was Dorcas.

Ruth sighed. She had just managed to claim some alone time and now she would have to go over to the wayward hen before she laid her egg in Father Donatello's garden clogs, which he left outside the rectory door.

Ruth scrambled down out of the tree and sprinted across the street. She was relieved to see that Father Donatello's car was gone. At least she wouldn't have to apologize for Dorcas's interloping while listening to him say how he loved all creatures. Ruth worried he meant he loved them with potatoes and gravy.

As she reached the rectory's front door, which faced the parking lot, Ruth couldn't see Dorcas anywhere. Where had she gone? The rain was harder now and her hair was dripping as she checked among the hen's favorite hostas, and the hydrangeas and the ferns that hugged the church foundation. That's when Ruth noticed the rectory door was ajar. Surely Dorcas wouldn't have gone inside. Would she? Maybe she wanted to get out of the rain.

Ruth went to the door and pushed it open a bit farther. "Dorcas," she whispered, sticking her head in. "Dorcas!"

There was no responding clucking. Ruth pushed the door open more. Why had Father Donatello left it open? It wasn't like him. He was very fastidious about locking up. He had to be. He had a cupboard full of wine and a village full of thirsty parishioners.

Ruth took a step inside the door. She had never been in the rectory before. She was in a wood-paneled foyer where a sturdy staircase wound its way up to the second floor on her right and a doorway to the left led into what looked like Father Donatello's office.

"Dorcas?" She felt odd standing there and was about to back out of the rectory when she heard a noise like something scraping coming from a closed door under the stairs Ruth figured it must lead to the basement. She paused, wondering if she were hearing things, but then the scratching noise happened again. Ruth wanted to leave because the door was closed — there was no way Dorcas could have gotten down there. Even if the basement door *had* been open, Dorcas couldn't have closed it behind her. Unless, Ruth thought, it *was* open, Dorcas went in and the wind slammed the door shut.

Ruth poked her head outside again, in case she could see the hen and not do what she was pretty sure she was about to do — go into the basement. The question of how much prison time you get for a break-and-enter only flickered across her mind as she opened the basement door.

"Dorcas?"

A flash of lightning and a crack of thunder made her jump, and she thought she heard a faint squawk from below. Dorcas hated storms.

Ruth tried the light switch and a dim light bulb came on, casting an orangey glow down in the room. She descended the wooden stairs, straining to hear the sound of chicken toes on concrete. Father Donatello's basement was surprisingly cluttered, with shelving units full of bins and boxes blocking her view. She figured it must all belong to the church because priests were supposed to live simply, weren't they?

Listening so intently for a cluck was giving her a headache. Dorcas was going to be locked inside the coop for a week for this. From the back corner came a scraping sound. Ruth made her way over quietly, so the hen wouldn't suddenly take off and lead Ruth on a chase around the crammed basement.

Then Ruth heard something that made her freeze mid-stride. A soft cough. Ruth knew the sounds chickens made — a cough wasn't one of them. Ruth lowered herself into a crouch. She bent over so she could peer under the shelves at floor level.

Please let there only be chicken legs, she pleaded inside her head.

But there wasn't. There was a shoe at the far end of the basement. A dark shoe that was now lifting off the ground as someone stepped quietly towards her.

Ruth couldn't breathe. She slowly inched along the shelving unit toward the wall, but there was nowhere to hide. As soon as the person in the shoe walked past that shelf, she would be caught. The sole of a shoe squeaked. Tears of terror gathered at the corners of her eyes. Then there was an intense flash of light and an immediate crash of thunder. The dim orange light bulb went black as the power went out. She had only seconds to escape. She crawled to the end of the aisle and just as she was about to stand and take off running back to the stairs, she heard a click and saw a white beam of light that looked like it came from a cellphone.

The arc of the beam only had to swing a bit to the right and she would be exposed. Her mind was in a panic — should she run, crawl back, try and knock the phone out of the person's hand and make a run for it? The light began to swing wider. She didn't know what to do. As the light came around and landed on her knee, Ruth let out a gasp. The light suddenly swung around wildly and there was a loud clatter of metal on the floor. In the darkness there was the furious flapping of wings, a throaty *brawqk* and sharp claws scraping floors, shelves, and likely, nefarious people lurking in the shadows.

"Aaaaaah," the shoe-person yelled in a deep voice and Ruth heard the pounding of footsteps across the basement, up the wooden stairs, and out.

Ruth almost wept with relief. Dorcas to the rescue. Again. The hen seemed to be making a habit of getting Ruth out of sticky situations. Maybe she wouldn't lock her up in the coop after all.

"Dorcas?"

Ruth desperately wanted to grab the hen and get out, but of course, now Dorcas had disappeared again. Ruth crawled forward in the darkness, swooping her arm out in front of her, hoping to encounter feathers, but there was nothing. When she put her hand back on the ground, it landed on a piece of cold metal. She pushed it to the side and figured she must be past the shelves and in the main aisle so she swung around to her right.

"OW!" Her head throbbed from banging it on a metal strut. She rubbed her head, knowing a big goose egg was forming. There was a soft answering cluck to the left, in the far corner of the basement.

"Farthest corner from the door," Ruth muttered, going back to her original plan to give Dorcas a time out when she got home. She stood up and moved forward gingerly, still rubbing her head. She felt her way down the aisle, calling to the hen every few steps. She was sure she had gone far enough that she was going to bang into the wall when, with a click, the light came on again. It took a second for Ruth to orient herself. She was indeed about to bang smack into an old wooden lectern in the corner. On a small table next to it were cans of furniture stripper, putty, rags, and stain. Ruth could see now that the lectern was in the middle of being restored. From the state of the dark wood, it looked old — ancient, even. Then she realized the dark wood was actually charred. This had been in a fire.

Ruth heard a soft coo. She peered around the lectern and there was Dorcas, sitting comfortably on the floor in a pile of rags. With a smug look, she got up and Ruth saw a brown egg nestled in the middle of the material.

"Nutty bird," Ruth said. She leaned over to pick up the egg, but it rolled next to the lectern. As she picked up the egg and put it in her jacket pocket, she saw it. The back of the lectern was hollow except for the area right up under the sloped ledge where books or papers rested. Tucked underneath seemed to be a built-in box or cabinet with a small keyhole on the left. Carved on the front panel of this lockbox was a mandala. The pattern looked just like the one of the back of the ugly hair picture.

Ruth felt the room spin slightly. She grabbed on to the lectern to not end up face first on the floor. The mandala. What was this design doing on an old, burned lectern? The answer came to Ruth in a rush. The lectern must be from the Old Parish Church. For some reason, it was saved from the fire. The dizziness passing, she tilted her head up underneath again and took a closer look at the carving. In the top right-hand corner, the wood was splintered and broken like someone was trying to pry the panel off. Ruth looked at the keyhole again. The size was about right. She pulled her key necklace up over her head and then tried the key in the lock.

It fit perfectly.

Shaking, just a little, she turned the key and pulled. With a creak, the panel swung open. For not the first time, Ruth wished she had a flashlight with her, or at least was allowed to have a cellphone so she could access the light on it. She put her hand in slowly, hoping there were no spiders or creepy crawlies. The box was about six inches square and the wood inside was smooth. She felt all the way back into the far corners and up the wall, but it was empty. With a sigh she closed the panel and locked it again. She felt a gentle peck on her ankle.

"You're right, Dorcas. Let's get out of here." She scooped up the hen and with one backward glance at the charred lectern, she headed for the stairs. As she got back to where she had almost been caught, she skidded to a stop in horror. The metal item the intruder had dropped lay on the floor — a crowbar. A shiver started on her scalp and traveled with lightning speed down her spine. She sprinted up the stairs not even stopping to pick up the crowbar in case the intruder was waiting for her upstairs, closed the basement door behind her, and scooted out the rectory door, closing that too.

As she carried Dorcas across the road, she did her best to control her breathing and look calm. After all, she told herself, everyone had seen her finding the wayward hen a million times all over town. No one would even notice.

But someone did notice.

❧ Chapter 24 ❧

"Ruth, breathe," Saul said at their emergency meeting under the bridge that afternoon. Ruth was shaking as she recounted her escapade in Father Donatello's basement.

"Breathe? BREATHE?" Ruth shouted.

"Shhhhhh!" Saul cautioned her.

"Sure, I'll just stand here and breathe while some maniac comes after me with a crowbar."

"You're sure it was the same guy as in your backyard?"

Ruth folded her arms. "Just how many people do you think run around with crowbars in Pinkerton?"

Saul rolled his eyes. "I'm just *asking*. And it sounds like he was down there before you, so he couldn't have brought the crowbar to attack you."

Ruth had to admit that Saul was annoyingly right. The intruder brought the crowbar for some other reason. And she thought she knew why.

"The lockbox. The lockbox with the carved mandala had damage up in the corner as if someone was trying to break into it."

"But it was empty, right?" Saul asked.

"Yes. Except for this." Ruth opened her palm to reveal a tiny flake.

"What is it?" Saul almost had his nose in her hand trying to see what it was.

"Gold."

Saul's head snapped back. "No. Really? Gold!"

"It was stuck to my hand after I checked out the lockbox. It had to have come from there."

Saul smiled. "So there *is* treasure. The ruby brooch must have been part of it too. And the gold was hidden there? In the rectory basement in a box under a lectern that Aunt Bea had the key to. But where is the treasure now? Did crowbar man get it?"

Ruth shook her head. "No. There was only a bit of damage on the corner. The lock was still intact. I think I interrupted him."

Saul tried to straighten up under the low bridge to stretch his cramped muscles, but hit his head on the concrete instead.

"If crowbar man didn't get it," Ruth said, "that must mean

it was already moved. But where? I think we need to figure out the importance of the mandala, and why we're finding it everywhere. Figuring out what Bea was hiding is sure to lead us to her killer."

"Right," Saul said. "The hair picture makes the same pattern on the back …"

"Ugly hair picture," Ruth corrected him.

"And it's on the lockbox in the old lectern that your key fits."

"I think I've seen it somewhere else," Ruth said. "Pass me your phone."

Saul pulled out his phone and handed it to her. She scrolled through the pictures. "Here. Look at this." On his phone screen was the image he took of the Old Parish Church in Bea's book on the history of Pinkerton.

Ruth pointed to the circular stained-glass window in the peaked wall above the church's front door. A pattern of lines, petals, and arcs radiated out from the circle in the center. There was no mistaking the pattern. It resembled the mandala on the back of the ugly hair picture and on the lectern in Father Donatello's basement.

"Yup, that's definitely the same design," Saul said.

"But what does it mean? Does it have something to do with the Templars? The treasure?"

Saul put his phone back in his pocket. "I don't know. I'll check it out when I get home. Dad freaked out over our phone data bill last month."

Ruth hated waiting, but there was nothing she could do. Unless … no, she shook her head slightly. She couldn't risk using her dad's computer.

"I'll get a hold of you as soon as I know anything. Dad has a deadline, so it might be a while before I can do a search online."

Ruth nodded and slipped out from under the bridge after she checked that the coast was clear.

Back in the house, Ruth kept her eyes straight ahead as she walked past her father's tiny office. It was a bad idea to look up the meaning of the mandala on the computer. Her dad would fret for days that his passwords had been hacked or something if he noticed an off-limits search.

"Not that he would," she muttered to herself. "Why would he, if he thinks no one else is using it? And he's at work. I could be in and out and he'd never even know." Turned out that Ruth could be very easily influenced by her own arguments, so much so that she waited until Abe left the kitchen with a drink and she slipped into the office.

She sat down at the computer and switched it on before she lost her nerve. The search bar came up. She typed as fast as she could.

Templar treasure design

Nothing of interest popped up.

Templar treasure pattern

The only results that came up were websites with conspiracy theories and hints at secret tunnels and documents. Ruth was pretty skeptical when it came to the Internet, ever since she found out that Emily Parsons was behind the really professional-looking website that dished out gossip and lies about the students at Robert Abram School. If Emily could pull that off, then any website could be full of fake reports and theories.

She tried searching images instead.

Templar treasure mandala

And partway down the page, there it was: a color image of a mandala that was almost an exact match of the one they had been finding. Ruth clicked on the link. At first, she wasn't sure what she was looking at. Then she realized it was a document written in French. Ruth strained to remember any of the basic French Madame Fogarty had tried to teach her, but was pretty sure "Do you know the way to the train station?" wouldn't help her right now.

Ruth got up from the chair and cracked open the office door. No one was in the kitchen and the TV was blaring from the den. It was a good thing a Godzilla marathon was running on the Sci-Fi Channel, because the printer clunked and whirred loudly. Ruth decided not to erase the browsing history because its absence would be more suspicious than hoping a few searches would be overlooked or buried after a few days. She grabbed the paper from the printer, closed the browser, and turned off the computer. She quietly slipped out of the office, grabbed the kitchen phone, and took it up to her room.

"Saul? Saul?"

"Ruth? Why are you whispering? I can barely hear you."

"I don't want my nosy brothers eavesdropping. I've found something. Is your dad home? Is the computer free?"

"Yeah, he's here. No, I can't use the computer yet; Dad has a deadline."

"Oh. How's your French?"

"*Très bien. Pourquoi?*"

"I hope that means good, because I need your help to translate a document. Can you meet me tonight at the coop?"

"I can't tonight. Dad is really stressed about this deadline and doesn't want to be disturbed at all, and he's expecting a package. I promised him I'd wait for it and let him know when it gets here."

"Can I come over, then?"

"*Bien sur.*"

Ruth didn't answer. This was when she regretted day-dreaming during French. "That means, yes, no?"

Saul laughed. "Yes."

"I'll be there around six."

"*Adieu*," Saul said.

"Show off," Ruth replied.

⮾ Chapter 25 ⮿

"Where did you find this?" Saul asked Ruth, peering at the document on his kitchen table. They kept their voices low so his father wouldn't hear them in his office upstairs.

"Online. I found a mandala almost the same as the ones we've been finding and it linked to this page." She looked at the image over his shoulder. "It looks old." She tried to be patient but failed. "What does it say?"

Saul ignored her for a few minutes, concentrating on the words.

"Saul, seriously, you're killing me here. What does it say?"

"It's part of the diary of a monk who lived in Montségur, France. He's talking about a nun who was a *Patrona*."

"What's a *Patrona*?"

"He says it means *protectress*, or *female defender*."

"Protectress of what?"

"It doesn't say." He read some more, mouthing the words he was trying to translate. "He says the mandala was the symbol for this line of women."

"Line?"

"It sounds like the responsibility of protecting whatever it was, was passed down from generation to generation. Each one was a Patrona, together they were Patronae, plural."

The words of Great-grandmother Hildie's will came back to Ruth:

As she is destined to carry the burden. Is that what she meant? Was she part of this lineage of Patronae?

"Do you think it's the treasure? Templar treasure? Is that what they could have been protecting?"

Saul shrugged. "Could be. I mean, the monk mentions the Templars a few times, and this is the part of France where the Templars were active."

Ruth was quiet.

"Something is bothering you," Saul said.

Ruth looked at the floor. "It just seems …" She gave a little sigh. "It seems like a lot of, I don't know, fuss. I mean, was it really necessary to have this whole line of people working together over centuries just to hide some necklaces and coins? Wouldn't a strong safe be just as effective?"

"The Templar treasure was more than a few trinkets. It

was worth millions. Billions, maybe. And from what I've read, it was no ordinary treasure, either. It wasn't just precious gems and metals, there was some secret too."

"What kind of secret?"

"Something someone didn't want to leak out."

"A secret worth protecting," Ruth said, mulling it over.

"A secret worth killing for," Saul said.

"Let me get this straight. You're saying Beatrice Payens was killed because she was protecting Templar treasure — a Templar secret? She is one in a long line of Patronae, and someone traced her or the treasure here to Pinkerton and murdered her for it? And somehow I'm next in line?"

Saul nodded.

A wave of fright washed over her. She didn't like this. She didn't want to be a part of this. It would be easy to deny everything they'd discovered. After all, it was pretty far-fetched. The sleepy village of Pinkerton was as far away from mysterious groups, hidden treasures, and deadly secrets as any place could be. That stuff belonged in books and movies, not real life. She could just close her mind to it all and go with the story that Bea slipped and fell into a river running fast and high because of spring rains and she left Ruth some knickknacks because she was eccentric. It would be so much easier. Ruth wouldn't have to worry about murderers roaming around the village or crowbar-carrying night crawlers, or what all those flowers meant.

"That reminds me, what about the flowers?" Ruth asked. "Are they a piece of this puzzle?"

"You know, Aunt Bea has this big book on flowers on the bookshelf. That can't be a coincidence, can it?"

"Nothing else has been," Ruth said. "Let's have a look."

Saul went to the built-in bookshelves in the living room and pulled down a thick, leather-bound book. The brown cover had the words *Barrett's Botany* etched on it in gold leaf. He brought it back to the kitchen.

"Looks like she read it a lot," Ruth said, touching the worn pages.

"Where should we start?"

"That's easy. Bea's favorite: roses."

Ruth knew red roses stood for love and romance, but what did Bea's pink roses mean? *Gratitude, grace, admiration, and joy*, the page read under pink roses. Ruth felt that summed up Bea, right there. It was getting dark outside and the print on the pages was faded.

"Can you turn on the light, Saul? It's getting hard to read this."

The kitchen light wasn't that strong so Saul got the little LED flashlight hanging by the back door.

"Did you know roses symbolized secrecy?" Saul asked. "Look here …" He trained the flashlight on the page so Ruth could read the section but instead of a bright white, light, it shone blue. "Shoot, sorry. I hit the switch for blacklight." The light shone white again.

"Saul," Ruth said quietly. "Do that again. Shine your blacklight on the page."

"Why?"

"Because it looked like something else was written there."

Saul switched back to blacklight and pointed it at the page. Words in Bea's distinctive scrawl appeared. Ruth stared intently at them:

Ruth, I have left you … Ruth burst into tears. It was like Bea was talking right to her, telling her goodbye.

Saul gave her a few moments and then said quietly, "What if that's not the whole message?"

"You think there's more?" Ruth sniffed and then hiccupped.

"I don't think she'd waste invisible writing just to tell you goodbye. She could have done that with an inscription at the front of the book."

Ruth thought about Bea's hat. "Check lilies."

The words were revealed under the blacklight: *to a secret*

"Secret? What secret? The secret of the Templar treasure?" Saul shrugged.

"Check forget-me-not," Ruth said.

for you to protect

"Those phrases don't make sense. There's got to be more. What other flowers were on her hat?" Saul asked.

"Solomon's seal," Ruth said. "Is there anything on the Solomon's seal page?"

A map

Saul did a quick check with the blacklight, but it seemed no other pages had writing. "If we put it in order, I think the message is:

Ruth, I have left you a map to a secret for you to protect."

∽ Chapter 26 ∽

Sleep wouldn't come to Ruth. Her mind spun and whirled trying to make sense of everything she and Saul had discovered. Bea *had* been trying to leave her a message. But the real question for Ruth was, why didn't Bea just tell her? Why did she leave clues and codes instead?

She asked Saul that same question when he showed up at her back door to pick up some fresh eggs for his dad. Ruth had volunteered to get them with him from the spare fridge in the garage so she could ask him in private.

"I think crowbar man is your answer," he said.

"What do you mean?"

"Well, if Bea suspected someone was on to her, she didn't want to paint a target on your back by making it obvious you were next in line. And now, despite her caution, that is exactly what has happened."

Ruth tried not to act like she was panicking. But she was. She didn't like the thought that someone was lying in wait for her. It was a waste of time, anyway, she thought because she didn't know anything about a hidden treasure or a powerful secret. Bea wrote in invisible ink in the flower book that she had left a map for Ruth, but Ruth didn't know where that was. And she had to wonder if Bea had made a mistake, and Ruth wasn't part of these protectresses, or Patronae. How would she know for sure?

"It'll be all right," Saul said as he left with the eggs.

Ruth was glad he seemed to be worried about her, but she was more concerned they figure out what Bea's secret was and who was after them. "Maybe check out the bookshelf again. It seems like Bea left a lot of clues there," she told him.

"I'll let you know if I find anything." Saul waved as he headed down the driveway.

Ruth went back in the house and decided to distract herself with *Anne of Green Gables*. She went into the den, lay back on the horsehair sofa and just got to the part where Diana got drunk on raspberry wine when Abe and George barreled in.

"Hey, can we have that picture?" Abe asked.

Ruth turned to look at where he was pointing. It was the ugly hair picture. Ruth was just about to tell them it was all theirs, so long as she never had to look at it again, when her eyes narrowed.

"Why?" It was always dangerous to give in to the requests of her brothers. Ruth still hadn't recovered from the time when she was five and they asked their mother for her kitchen mandolin, which they turned into a guillotine and then demanded ransom from Ruth to save her dolls' heads.

George piped up. "Abe says we're going to clone a monster from that hair. For sure there's woolly mammoth or saber-toothed tiger DNA in there."

"No there isn't, you juvenile delinquents. That's human hair." Then Ruth stopped, a chill racing through her veins as she realized the implication of what they were saying. She jumped up, shooing her brothers out of the room. She took down the picture and looked at it again. The hair strands were all different colors and thicknesses. They were all from different people. It wasn't just a craft some Victorian ladies did to fill their time ... this was more than that. Hair contained human DNA and DNA was passed down from generation to generation. This hair picture was a DNA trail. This could prove that Bea wasn't mistaken, and that as the first girl born into her dad's family in two generations, she was the *one destined to carry the burden.* This was the family tree Ruth was looking for and it had been right under her nose or, more accurately, just above her head this whole time.

"Bea," she said, tracing her finger over the petal at the top that had been glued and not sewn. It looked like it had been done in a hurry. "Because she knew she was running out of time," Ruth said quietly.

She began to hang the picture back up, but then thought better of it. Her brothers might still think they could do experiments on it. She took it, and her book, up to her room. She looked around for a suitable place for such an important artifact, but the fact was, it was still a bit creepy and ugly and it might still give her nightmares if it were hanging on her wall.

"Sorry Bea," she said as she laid it on top of a bin of her winter sweaters on the shelf in her closet. She plunked herself down on her bed, opened her book, and tried to read again. It was no use. Anne's trouble with Gilbert Blythe in school couldn't hold her attention and she left the book and headed outside to her maple tree. Nestled hidden among the branches, she thought about Bea's message in the flower book: *I have left a map to a secret for you to protect.*

Ruth tried to make sense of it all. It was looking like she really *was* one of the Patronae and Bea was a distant relative. She didn't feel like a Patrona. But then, she wasn't sure what being a Patrona would feel like. Secretive? Powerful? Maybe this is why she felt invisible? Maybe invisibility was a trait of the Patronae who had a deep secret to keep?

"I wish you were here," Ruth whispered, thinking of Bea. "Or that you had explained this all to me when you were."

"Are you all right?"

Ruth almost fell off the branch at the voice. "Who … who said that?"

She looked down to see her brother George below, looking up. She was devastated to realize that her hiding place had been discovered.

In a flash, George scaled the tree and took a seat on the next branch over. "Hey, this is a pretty nice view."

"How did you know I was up here?" Ruth asked.

George snorted. "I've always known you were here. Of course, you've missed the salamander count again this year."

"You've always known I was here? And you didn't rat me out?" she asked, incredulously.

George shrugged. "Just figured you needed some time to yourself."

Not so invisible, Ruth thought. "Um … thanks for not saying anything." They sat in silence for a moment. "Can I ask your advice?"

He nodded.

"When you're playing your video games, the quest ones, how do you figure out where to go and what to do next?"

"I look for clues."

"What if you don't understand the clues?"

"You just have to look at them in a different way. The info

is all there." George smiled, climbed down the tree, and took off for the house.

Ruth went over the clues Bea had left her in her mind, including the strange inscription on the key. CT VI 3922 she thought smugly — Saul wasn't the only one who could remember details. But what did it mean? Ruth thought about Saul's insistence that an intruder was coming into his house. What if he wasn't paranoid? *Look at the clues in a different way. Okay*, Ruth thought. *What were the targets? His closet, the basement, and the bookshelves.*

The bookshelves! Ruth realized that a lot of answers had come from there: the book on the history of Pinkerton and the book of flowers. *Maybe George wasn't such a pest after all*, she thought.

Ruth scrambled down from the tree and ran over to Saul's. She didn't care who saw; she knew they were running out of time.

"Hello Mr. Rolls. Is Saul in?" Ruth asked, out of breath when his father answered the door.

"Yeah, sure. Come in." Mr. Rolls held the door open for her. Saul came down the stairs at the sound of her voice.

"I just came down for coffee," Mr. Rolls said, looking from one to the other. "Well, I had better get back to work." He took his mug up the stairs, not looking back.

"You look, um, frazzled," Saul said. "What's going on?"

"I think I know where the last clue leads."

"What last clue?"

"The inscription on the key. That's the only clue that we don't understand because I finally figured out the ugly hair picture."

"It created the mandala on the back with the threads, right?"

"Right, but everything seems to have two meanings. My brothers inadvertently unlocked the other part. It's human hair. It's a DNA family tree of the women of the Patronae."

"An ugly family tree?"

"Exactly. It's what ties me to all the other women that came before me."

"That's creepy."

"Yeah, kinda. But at least it makes sense."

"So you've figured out the key now?"

"No, but I think I know where to look."

"And that is …"

"The bookshelf. Bea loved books and we've already found some answers there. And you also said you thought someone had been going through them … that they were out of order."

"Hmmm. Show me the inscription again."

CT VI 3922

They walked to the bookshelves in the Bea's living room and scanned the spines of the books looking for C and T.

"*Curses and Threats: A History of Wiccan Rebels*?" Saul asked.

"I don't think so," Ruth said. "How about *Coffee Treats*?"

"Nah. Bea was definitely a tea drinker. That was probably a gift." Saul moved on to the second bookcase. "Here's one: *Cow Tipping: A Beginner's Guide*."

"I can't imagine that being relevant," Ruth said. Her finger glided over some leather-bound classics. "Wait! This must be it: *The Canterbury Tales*. Bea told me once that it was one of her favorites." Ruth pulled it off the shelf. "And look, it says Volume I. That must be the 'V-I'"

"So 3922 must be the page number?"

"No, it's not that big." Ruth opened the book and scanned the pages. "But it looks like the lines are numbered. Line 3922 …" She flipped until she came to the right spot and read Bea's clue.

❧ Chapter 27 ❧

*T*her gooth a brook and over that a brigge.

"Huh?" Ruth said. "Is that English?"

"Probably some sort of Old English. There's a translation here on the side," Saul said, pointing. "It means: *There goes a brook and over that a bridge.*"

They looked at each other.

"The bridge!" they both said in unison.

"Bea told me in her letters that she was on the SCBRC — the Spencer Creek Bridge Reconstruction Committee."

"That must be where the treasure is." Ruth punched Saul in the arm. "Well, don't just stand there, let's go!"

Ruth took off out the back door and headed for the bridge. She could hear Saul's footsteps behind her. The road through town was empty. Maybe they would get lucky, Ruth thought, and no one would see them.

Ruth stopped when she got to the bridge. So *where* exactly

would it be? The top of the bridge was too exposed. It had to be underneath.

Ruth scrambled down the bank and didn't even care that her socks and shoes were wet from splashing through the shallow creek. She ducked under the concrete bridge and stopped. She had been under there so many times trying to get Dorcas and had never noticed anything that could be a hiding spot for a treasure. Saul joined her with splash.

"Do you think it's in the creek?" Saul asked.

Ruth shook her head. "Whatever it was would be damaged by the moisture."

"Do you think it's in the ceiling, right under the road? We could have been walking right over it."

Ruth looked around, trying to find a spot in the smooth concrete that would hint at a cavity. "It all looks too perfect," she said. "No cracks, no bumps, no obvious repairs."

Saul slowly turned, looking at every inch. "What about that?"

Ruth looked where he was pointing. "That's just the construction plaque," she said. She stepped forward to take a closer look. "You know, it says who built it ..." Her voice trailed off as she read the words for the first time:

Corporation of Teeswater
Veterans Institute
Branch 3922

"I don't believe it," she said.

"What?" Saul asked coming over and standing beside her.

"Look at the first letters of the inscription: CT VI 3922" Ruth looked at him with wide eyes. "This is it."

"Seems too much of a coincidence." Saul shook his head. "There probably isn't even a Veterans Institute in Teeswater."

"You told me Bea was on the Bridge Reconstruction Committee though, right? She could have made some changes that no one would question — including installing a fake plaque."

"I guess. But how do we get it off and see behind it?"

Ruth ran a hand over the brass plaque. The rivets were flush with the plaque and looked tight and impossible to remove. As her fingers ran over the edge, she noticed something in the small crest in the bottom right-hand corner. The design almost hid the fact that the middle was a hole. A hole of a peculiar shape and size. A shape and size she knew well.

She pulled the key on the chain out from under her t-shirt and then put the key into the hole. And like before in Father Donatello's basement, it fit perfectly. She turned the lock and pulled. The plaque swung open on invisible hinges.

Ruth expected the space to be empty, just like the box built in under the lectern. But this wasn't empty. Even in the darkness under the bridge Ruth and Saul could see a box sitting inside. Ruth reached in pulled it out.

They gasped.

It was about the size of a box of cookies, but this was no ordinary container. The outside shimmered even in the dim light under the bridge. It was made of gold and the sides and top were decorated with red, blue, green, and purple gems in a pattern that swirled and spiraled. It was surprisingly heavy too. Ruth gently lifted the lid. Inside was lined with a rich copper that was etched and carved into a parade of animals and plants that circled the inner band. And that wasn't all. In the middle was a pile of tightly wound scrolls. They looked old and brittle and Ruth worried that if she touched them, they would break apart.

"I can't believe we found it," Saul said. "And the scrolls must be the secret. Take the top one out carefully so we can see what it says."

"I would prefer it if you didn't. Now pass the box over to me."

Ruth and Saul spun around at the sound of the voice.

Standing behind them was Mr. Weeks. His face was twisted into a nasty sneer.

Ruth froze. Mr. Weeks? He had always seemed so friendly and harmless. Well, not today. He held out one hand to take the box and the other hand moved into the leather satchel strapped across his chest and pulled out a crowbar. She shuddered involuntarily. Mr. Weeks took a step toward her.

"Give. Me. The. Box."

Ruth instinctively held the gold box closer. She knew she now had the responsibility of keeping the treasure and the secret safe. Hundreds of years of women had successfully kept it hidden and safe and here she was, on her first day on the job and she was already in danger of losing it.

"This doesn't belong to you," she said through gritted teeth.

"It will in a minute," Mr. Weeks said calmly. "Now hand it over. You don't want me to have to persuade you, do you?" he said, gently swaying the crowbar.

A chill ran down her spine.

"You need to leave." It was Saul. He had stepped in front of her to shield her.

"Stupid boy," Mr. Weeks rasped. The crowbar came up and before he could strike him, Ruth pushed Saul out of the way. Saul slipped in the mud but looked like he was about to regain his footing when Mr. Weeks jabbed at him with his elbow, sending Saul into the side of the bridge support. Saul struck his head on the concrete wall and slid to the ground where he lay still.

Ruth tried to scream, but nothing came out of her mouth. Saul moaned on the ground and Ruth was relieved to hear him. A sickening smile spread over Mr. Weeks's face. He lifted the crowbar again, but before he could swing it, an ear-splitting squawk erupted and echoed off the concrete. A flurry of feathers and claws and beak filled the space between Ruth and Mr. Weeks. It was all Ruth needed. She spun around, sped out the other side of the bridge, and sprinted down the creek. She could hear the splashing of Mr. Weeks following her. Her heart was thudding against her ribcage; her breath came in ragged gasps. The splashing footsteps behind her seemed to be getting closer. She knew she had to get away from the creek because running through the water was slowing her down. She tried to jump up the right-hand bank toward Mrs. Gorgonzola's house, but the bank was steeper on that side and bushes lined the top of it. She lost her footing and for a terrifying second, she stalled and Mr. Weeks gained on her. She gave up that idea and took a few more long strides through the water and then jumped up the left-hand bank. She took off across the field.

Ruth was breathing really hard now and she could feel her speed slowing. Worse than that, she was heading away from Pinkerton and any hope of help. She did her best to weave and turn, trying to shake Mr. Weeks, but she could hear him keeping up to her. She didn't realize until too late that the path she had been following led straight to the bank of the Teeswater River. She could see the water now, swollen and angry from the two days of rain they had had.

Ruth knew there was a path somewhere up ahead that led

away from the river, heading the back way to the ruins of the Old Parish Church, that she and Portia had followed back to town. If she could get to it, maybe she could sprint ahead of Mr. Weeks and have a few minutes out of his sight to disappear down the tunnel. She could just see the break in the bushes where the path was when she slipped on some acorns and fell to the ground. The box flew out of her hands and landed on the gravel just out of reach.

The fall caused the wind to be knocked out of her. As she lay there rolling and gasping for air, willing her lungs to fill again, she saw Mr. Weeks's shoes walk around her and over to the box. He bent down and picked it up.

Ruth was able to take a few shallow breaths and rolled up onto her knees. Mr. Weeks wasn't even looking at her; he couldn't take his eyes off the box. In the sunlight, the gold glowed even brighter and the gems sparkled brilliantly. Her breathing easing, Ruth staggered to her feet. That caught Mr. Weeks's attention. He put the box carefully in the satchel as he pulled out the crowbar again.

"She did a good job hiding your identity, you know. She never gave you up even right up to the end."

Ruth gulped. "The end? Then you … then she …?"

"Fell in the river and drowned. Yes. Saved me the trouble of killing her, not that it worried me. It would have been easy. Old lady like that. I told her I'd spare her life if she gave me the treasure and told me who was next. But she wouldn't. Seems she'd rather die than give you up. So she did. And it didn't matter in the end anyway. I figured it out. And now I have both you and the treasure."

"You'd kill over a stupid box?" Ruth said, anger at his callousness toward the death of her dear friend.

"This is not just a box, which will fetch a big enough price on the black market. No, it's the scrolls. The secret."

"What secret?"

Mr. Weeks laughed. "Didn't anyone tell you? Didn't the box give it away? The inside is copper, but the outside ..." his hand caressed the satchel that held the box "... is pure gold."

Ruth scrunched up her face. "Seriously? This is about turning copper into gold?" She forced herself to laugh. "That's ridiculous. Old alchemists tried to turn lead into gold, not copper."

"And that's why it never worked. But the scrolls ... the scrolls hold the formula." He smiled that creepy smile again. "There are just two more small details I need to take care of — that wannabe honorable knight knocked unconscious under the bridge back there, and ... the last Patrona." His eyes bored into her.

Ruth took a step back, wishing she had run the other direction, into town instead of way out here where no one could hear her. She took another step back. Mr. Weeks was forcing her to move closer to the edge of the river.

"Don't bother my dear. You're no match for me. Fitting, isn't it, that you will go the same way as Beatrice … sinking into the river."

"I can swim," Ruth said testily.

Mr. Weeks laughed. It wasn't a warm laugh like her father's, but a cold hollow sound.

"Not unconscious you won't."

"Look, you got your prize, just leave." Even to her own ears, Ruth could hear her voice shake.

"I'm not taking any chances. I've seen enough mystery shows to know that one loose thread can unravel everything. If it makes you feel any better, it will be quick."

He lifted the crowbar. She backed up again. She was getting so close to the edge of the river that she could hear the whoosh as the water ran by. Mr. Weeks stepped toward her. In this weird moment where everything seemed to be moving in slow motion, she thought how she had let Bea down and wondered if this is how Bea felt right before the river swept her away.

Chapter 28

The crowbar was raised high and Ruth instinctively raised her arms to shield her head from the blow when, out of the long grass on her left, a pink mass burst out and slammed into Mr. Weeks, knocking him sideways right to the edge of the river. He teetered for a moment, arms flailing, trying to regain his footing, but the crowbar in his arm was heavy and its weight was what finally tipped him over. He landed in the fast-moving water with a big splash. The angry river swept him away downstream, as he yelled and tried to fight the current and swim to shore. He was out of view in no time. And with him went the box.

Ruth smiled at Mr. Weeks's attacker who was now rooting around at her feet and grunting softly. Portia. The hungry pig seemed to be relieved that the stranger was away from her thick carpet of acorns and she began gorging herself on the crunchy treat.

Ruth bent down and scratched between the pig's ears with shaky hands. "Good girl. And thanks."

Portia grunted and gave a sloppy smile.

Ruth left the pig feasting on her prize as she ran back into town and the bridge to find Saul. She felt horrible that she had left him there, but it wasn't like she had a choice. She ducked under the bridge.

"Saul?"

A moan answered her. She ran over to him where he was still lying on the soggy ground. "Are you okay? Oh please be okay."

Saul held his head as he sat up. "Yeah, I think so. But I've got a massive bump forming. Thanks for pushing me, by the way."

"Hey, would you rather have your skull split in two by a crowbar?"

Saul slowly shook his head. "I wasn't being sarcastic. Thank you for pushing me. I'd rather have a concussion than … than …" He didn't need to finish. "And I'm sorry I wasn't more help. What happened? When I came to, you were both gone. Did Mr. Weeks run off with the box?"

"No. Just stealing the treasure and the secret wasn't enough for him. He wanted to get rid of all the evidence of his crime. And by evidence, I mean you and me."

"So how did you get away?"

Ruth told Saul how Mr. Weeks had chased her to the river and confessed to killing Bea. She could feel the tears pricking at her eyes. Then she told him how Portia had saved her from the same fate as Bea because Mr. Weeks was standing on her acorns.

"But I couldn't save the secret," Ruth said, her shoulders sagging. "Some Patrona I was. I managed to protect the treasure for all of thirty seconds."

"Mr. Weeks was dangerous and evil. Bea knew that more than anyone. And at least you're still here." Saul gave her a wide smile.

A warm flush spread through her. "Come on, let's get you back to your house and dose you up with some pain meds."

Saul moved very slowly as he got to his feet.

Ruth saw the still-open cavity with the plaque swinging on the hinges. She slammed it shut as hard as she could out of frustration at her failure. It banged on the concrete wall, making a cracking sound, and bounced open again.

"Uh oh. I think I broke it."

"You can't break a concrete bridge by slamming a little metal plaque. They're built to withstand fully loaded trucks. Let me see."

Saul trained his phone light over the cavity. "I don't see anything damaged. Are you sure you heard a crack?"

Ruth rolled her eyes and took the phone from him. "Let

me look." She trained the light over the inside of the hole. "See, there at the back, right in the top right corner, a crack. And …" She stopped, still shining the light on the back wall of the hole. "Okay, tell me I'm not imagining things. Tell me you see something carved in the back wall."

Saul took the light and looked. He glanced at her. "It looks like: SCBRC. Why would the back wall have the Reconstruction Committee's name on it?"

Ruth reached in and felt around the seams of the back wall. "The whole thing is loose. It's a false wall. I think I can move it." She scraped and pulled inch by inch until she could feel the whole stone move. She got her fingers behind it and pulled it out.

"Here, let me see." Saul held up the stone for a closer look at the initials carved on the front, while Ruth got a view of the back.

"You remember how everything had a double meaning?" Ruth asked him.

"Yeah. And?"

"Turn the stone over."

On the back was a deeply carved, intricate mandala. It was the same pattern as the one that stood for the line of Patronae, but this one had strange symbols in the different geometric circles and arcs. The deeply etched middle circle's symbol was lined with gold. One of the symbols in a bottom right arc was lined with copper.

"I don't believe it," Ruth whispered.

"What? What is it?" Saul asked.

"Mr. Weeks told me the Templar's secret was a formula to turn copper into gold. He said it was on the scrolls in the box. But it isn't. I don't know what is on those scrolls, but it's not the formula." Ruth pointed at the mandala. "*This* is the formula."

"The box must have been a decoy," Saul said, laughing. "Good old Aunt Bea. So clever. She hid the formula on the back of a simple stone. You didn't fail after all."

Ruth smiled. Then worry quickly returned. "Mr. Weeks might come back at any time. What should we do with this?"

"I don't think it will be safe in either of our houses. Someone could stumble upon it or the house could burn down …" Saul said.

"You're always so cheery," she said. "Actually, I think the safest place is back where it was. Even if Mr. Weeks could figure out this fast that the scrolls were a decoy, he'd never think that the real formula was in here. It looks empty to anyone who could even find a way to open it without the key."

Ruth was reluctant to part with the secret now that she

had it. The responsibility was almost overwhelming. But the truth was, she couldn't think of a safer place. "Help me put the stone back, then," she said.

They wedged the stone back in place and filled the cracks as best they could with sand and gravel. Then, Ruth locked the plaque into place. "Let's get out of here."

They hurried back to Saul's house where Ruth made sure his dad knew Saul might have a concussion. Mr. Rolls had Saul ice the lump on his head and assured Ruth he would keep an eye on him.

"Call me when you get home," Saul said quietly as she headed for the door.

Ruth nodded.

She walked the most obvious route right down the main street back to her house, hoping lots of people were around. It felt safer than cutting through the woods. She felt instant relief when she saw Mrs. Gorgonzola sitting in her front window. She even waved at her. A confused Mrs. Gorgonzola lifted a hand to give a small wave back.

Back home, Ruth took the phone into her room and called Saul to let him know she was home and to ask him an important question. "Do I tell my parents what happened? I mean, a killer is on the loose!"

There was silence on the other end of the line for a moment. "I don't know how we'd explain why Mr. Weeks would do such a thing without telling them why. And we can't divulge anything about the treasure."

"I know. But what if Mr. Weeks comes back and tries again?"

"Why would he? He thinks he's got what he wanted. He's probably on another continent by now."

In the end, they agreed Ruth should casually mention to her parents that she saw Mr. Weeks on the banks of the Teeswater River, looking drunk and wondered if he was okay. Then they could urge someone to report him missing. Then the police could track him down and hopefully let them know he was far, far away. In the meantime, Ruth should try and find out if her parents, or more specifically her dad, might already know about the Patronae. Then she could confide in him about Bea and Mr. Weeks.

"Ruth, are you okay?' her dad asked as she went downstairs and into the kitchen for a drink. "You're trembling."

Ruth nodded, but it was just dawning on her how close she had come to not coming home. Ever.

"You're sweating too."

"I'm fine, Dad, really," Ruth said, taking a big gulp of water and trying to still her hands. He didn't seem totally convinced, but he went back to reading his book.

Ruth didn't even know how to begin. She decided the direct approach was best.

"Why didn't you ever tell me about Grandmother Hildie?" she asked.

Her father looked up in surprise and his eyes opened wide. "Where did you hear about her?"

Ruth tried to look nonchalant. "I overheard something at the family reunion. Aunt Lily said Grandmother Hildie gave us this property. Why us?"

Her father rubbed his chin. "She had a thing about girls in the family. Don't know why. Wanted to do something special for us seeing as you came along — first girl in two generations." He shrugged. "I wasn't about to say no to a free house."

Ruth paused, wondering if he really didn't know about the Patronae. "She didn't say any more than that in her will?"

"Any more about what? The house? No … my brothers weren't too happy about how her estate was divided. Not happy at all. In fact, they threatened to take me to court. They didn't though, when they found out that whoever got the house had to actually live in it and not sell it out of the family. None of them wanted to settle way out here."

"Why didn't you say any of this when I asked you about your family tree for my project?"

"To be honest, there was so much anger and nasty arguments over the will that I broke ties with the family. For good. Just as well for you to forget them all."

Not likely, Ruth thought.

⚓ Chapter 29 ⚓

Ruth realized she still didn't know if she could confide in her dad or what he might know of *the burden* mentioned in the will. So the next morning Ruth tried again. "How well did you know Beatrice Payens?" she asked him as she toasted a frozen waffle. She wondered if he realized Grandmother Hildie's maiden name was also Payens and made the connection.

"Not well. She already lived in that house when we moved here. Nice lady, though."

"What about Mr. Weeks?" Just saying the name made Ruth's heart pound.

"He moved here about ten years ago. Why?"

Ruth wasn't sure what to tell him. Part of her wanted to just blurt it all out, hope he believed her, and feel safe again. "Oh, just um …"

She didn't know what words to use. Before she could stammer something out, her mother burst through the back door. "Anton, you won't believe what I just heard at the Gas 'n' Go. It seems Mr. Weeks was pulled from the Teeswater River down near Beamsville."

Her father looked at Ruth. "We were just talking about him."

"Yeah, weird, huh?" Ruth said, pouring syrup on her waffle.

Her father smiled and nodded, then turned to her mom. "So what happened?"

"Details are sketchy. Harriet Ings heard this from her cousin Pamela who heard it from her neighbor, whose husband is a volunteer firefighter, who heard it from the night shift. Word is he was nearly drowned when they dragged him out."

"Are they sure it's him?" Ruth said, trying not to look as frantic as she felt.

"Oh, there's no doubt. According to Phyllis's cousin's neighbor's husband's coworkers, they found his passport on him. I'm sure we'll get all the rest of the details on the news tonight."

Ruth gulped down her waffle and slipped out the back door while her parents were arguing over which news program would have the best coverage. Ruth ran over to Saul's house, still looking over her shoulder as she couldn't quite believe she wasn't in danger any more. She knocked on the back door and practically dragged Saul outside by the arm when he answered it.

"Did you hear?" she blurted.

Saul shook his head.

"Mr. Weeks is still on the loose!"

"Really?" Then Saul saw Ruth's expression. He put his hands on her shoulders. "It's going to be okay. We'll go to the police and tell them what happened. You'll be safe." He pulled her into a quick hug.

Ruth nodded and gulped.

"But what about the box?" he asked.

"I don't know yet. This all came through the grapevine. I guess we'll have to wait for the details on the news."

They were both quiet for a while.

When they stepped back, Ruth said, "Thank you for trying to protect me from Mr. Weeks."

Saul smiled and bowed. "All in the line of duty."

Ruth laughed and realized Saul wasn't the least bit annoying anymore. They agreed to meet at the coop that night, just for old times' sake.

"Did you watch the news?" Saul asked her that evening when he got there.

"No, I couldn't bear to," Ruth said.

"Well, you don't have to worry about Mr. Weeks."

"What do you mean?"

"They said when they checked his ID, that he had outstanding warrants for his arrest. Some kind of industrial espionage and fraud."

"Did they mention the box?"

"Nope. All he had was his passport but no luggage of any kind. I think they would have mentioned it, if he did. They wondered if he was going on a trip."

Ruth snorted. "Yeah, straight to a copper mine."

"So, are you going to replace the wooden box with another decoy under the bridge in case someone else figures out the clues and finds the spot?"

Ruth thought about it for a moment. "I don't see how they could. The frog is empty, and I'm keeping the key close to me. The ugly hair picture isn't even on our wall anymore; it's in my closet. And the gloves are just stuffed in my night table drawer. And besides, you said you burned the letter naming the items Bea said to give to me, so no one would even link them. There's really nothing else ..."

"Except this," Saul said, pulling the flower book out from behind his back. "I think *you* should keep it. After all, the message in it was meant for you."

Ruth took the book and rubbed her hand over the leather cover. "Thanks," she said.

"What about the formula? Thinking of trying your own

experiments? Try to turn some copper into gold? You could change your family's whole future."

Ruth thought about it. A quick image of horses, chickens, and the Pyramids flitted across her mind. "No. It's too dangerous. What would happen if I suddenly showed up with gold nuggets? Instant suspicion, especially if there are more like Mr. Weeks out there. We don't know if he was alone or if there are more suspicious Templar treasure hunters. And what if that formula got into the wrong hands? Can you imagine what someone who was truly evil would do with unlimited wealth? No, this has remained a secret for a reason."

Saul nodded, although Ruth thought he looked a little disappointed.

"Besides, I still have the brooch."

"I wouldn't flash that around, either," he said.

They parted ways and Ruth went back into the house. Her parents and brothers were all watching a movie in the living room so she sought some solace in her room. She went to her closet and got down the ugly hair picture. It was still ugly, she thought, but now it held a deeper meaning for her. She looked at the last little petal that was made from the tiny braid of hair that had been glued on. A few strands came loose as she gently ran a finger over it. She pictured Bea quickly adding her own hair to this amazing line of women.

Ruth sat on her bed and undid the tabs on the frame and took the backing off. For the first time she was grateful that her mother had made her learn to sew on any buttons that had ripped off her clothes. She took out a needle, some brown thread, and scissors. She slowly picked off the thick globs of glue off Bea's hair braid and then neatly sewed it in place, copying the other petals so her stitches matched the pattern on the back.

She turned the picture over and saw with satisfaction that Bea's petal was as it should be. Then smiling broadly, Ruth re-threaded the needle, took the scissors, and cut a small lock of her own hair. Tying the end with thread, she made a thin braid, fashioned it into a loop, and carefully sewed it beside Bea's in the hair flower, taking her place among the Patronae.

Acknowledgements

I stumbled across the real hamlet of Pinkerton after making a wrong turn on a country road. It was such a quiet, peaceful place that I immediately began to imagine what quirky characters might live there and what deep secrets they could be keeping. *Swept Away* grew out of that serendipitous discovery.

Many thanks go to my critique group, BAM, for their immeasurable help and support: Karen Bass, Lynn Leitch, Jennifer Maruno, Sharon McKay, Sylvia McNicoll, Anitha Robinson, Deborah Serravalle, and Claudia White. There was no character inconsistency too slight, no plot hole too small, no shift in POV too subtle for them to catch.

Thanks, too, to the wonderful team at Dancing Cat Books who worked on this book with me, especially my editor, Barry Jowett, and copyeditor, Sarah Jensen.

Many thanks to illustrator, Julie McLaughlin, for her

amazing cover. I love how it captures the mood and details of the story.

And last but not least, thanks to Alex, Alysha, Chelsey, Pat, Nathan, and Haley. You keep me grounded, hopeful, and looking forward. Most of all, heartfelt thanks to Craig, who is always up for a wrong turn that leads to an adventure.

Natalie Hyde is the author of both fiction and non-fiction for middle-grade and young adult readers. Her works include *Saving Armpit, Mine!*, and *Up the Creek,* and her books have received award nominations in both Canada and the US. Hyde is her family's genealogist — the "keeper of the bones" — and has traced her father's family back to the 1700s in Canada. She currently lives in Flamborough, Ontario.

We acknowledge the sacred land on which Cormorant Books operates. It has been a site of human activity for 15,000 years. This land is the territory of the Huron-Wendat and Petun First Nations, the Seneca, and most recently, the Mississaugas of the Credit River. The territory was the subject of the Dish With One Spoon Wampum Belt Covenant, an agreement between the Iroquois Confederacy and Confederacy of the Ojibway and allied nations to peaceably share and steward the resources around the Great Lakes. Today, the meeting place of Toronto is still home to many Indigenous people from across Turtle Island. We are grateful to have the opportunity to work in the community, on this territory.

We are also mindful of broken covenants and the need to strive to make right with all our relations.